Telegraph Hill

John F. Nardizzi

Merrimack
MEDIA

Paperback ISBN: 978-1-939166-11-1
Library of Congress Control Number: 2013936631

A Merrimack Media edition

For Stacie, who walked the city hills and nudged me to write it all down.

Dedicated to the memory of Jean Roberts, an Oakdale teacher who believed all that is gold does not glitter.

This is a work of fiction. Names, characters, businesses, organizations, places, events and incidents either are the product of the author's imagination or are used fictitiously. Any resemblance to actual persons, living or dead, events, or locales is entirely coincidental.

www.johnnardizzi.com

Telegraph Hill

JOHN F. NARDIZZI

Chapter 1

As night slouched on, the flesh and drug trade simmered at the intersection of Turk and Jones. Johnny Cho smoked a cigarette on the fire escape of the Senator Hotel. Johnny could have afforded a better room than the Senator; he was now earning huge sums of cash. Saving like only an immigrant can save, scraping money from every hungry minute.

Two men watched him from the shadows of the alley. They turned away and walked to Eddy Street, waiting for the call. One man tapped his jacket. Ready for the wet work. The men turned left on Leavenworth Street.

Johnny glanced at his watch: 10:33 PM. Across the street, graffiti on a brick wall—'Plastic people are cute.' He didn't understand the reference. Bodies lurched on the sidewalk, glowing in the neon lights of porn shops—crack whores, johns, dealers, trannies, junkies. Some didn't move at all, sprawled on greasy sidewalks.

His triad owned these sidewalks. They operated three massage parlors in the city's Tenderloin district: Crystal Massage, The Golden Lotus, and Tokyo Spa. All were fronts for prostitution. The world's oldest profession had a centuries-old lineage in the city. If not exactly accepted, the profession at least had carved out a certain measure of grungy respect. The massage parlors operated openly, signs beckoning over restaurants, ads in local papers. They generated substantial fees on their own, but as cash businesses, their value as money makers paled in comparison to their main function: laundering a steady torrent of drug money. And because of the triad's interest in developing new cash businesses, the massage parlors were earning him a very respectable living.

Johnny had left Hong Kong with a group of refugees when he was fourteen. They drifted for weeks across the Pacific on a chunk of rotten wood someone had the balls to call a boat. Eight dead bodies later, he made it to Los Angeles. Since then, he had come a long way from washing dishes in grubby Chinatown restaurants. First, a runner for the numbers, a trusted doorman. Then bigger assignments — jobs issued with a whisper, or on a dirty slip of paper, coded, you never knew the whole deal. Follow the man to see which apartment he enters at 10:30 PM. Get the address of the girl with the purple hat who works at the bank.

Then came other tasks, things he didn't talk about.

The feuding bosses of the major triads had met earlier that day, twenty-four men in total: bosses, favored lieutenants, and bodyguards hiding behind sunglasses. They talked over a long lunch at a big downtown hotel, ordering dim sum and cold beer, posturing and blowing cigarette smoke at each other. Johnny found the negotiations tiresome. He wanted some time away. A bit of a risk coming to the Senator Hotel with the girls — he usually went to one of the triad houses. But he did not want to be disturbed tonight, and he would have been recognized at the Lotus. He was not in the mood to listen to complaints. So, the Senator Hotel had been pressed into service once again. He'd dine alone too, if he could help it. Tomorrow promised another day of endless meetings.

He watched the street action, reaching absentmindedly for another cigarette. He was out. Where was the girl? She had gone inside over five minutes ago — still no smokes.

He heard a click in the alley. He looked down and saw a wooden door open into the passageway. The cement walkway gleamed, slick from an earlier rain. Two men slid inside. They walked past trash barrels into the shadows.

Johnny stared. One of the men looked up, and met his eye. The man muttered something. Then the men crouched and sprang toward the rear of the building.

Johnny shivered a bit, a spade dragging across cold stones. One of the men reached the iron fire escape. Hunching low, he took two steps at a time.

Johnny didn't like this at all. Reached down and felt a sickness in his gut — the snub .38 was in his jacket.

He sprang back from the edge of the railing and moved toward the battered steel door. He yanked the door handle — it was locked. He smashed his fist on the door, jammed his face near the small square window. One of the girls looked up, startled. He saw the other girl, the blond, packing her bag near the bathroom. For a second, his eyes met those of the blond, and he drew in her frightened complicity. Fucking whore — she set him up! He watched as she turned away, shouting something to the other girl.

Bracing against the rail, Johnny slammed his shoulder against the door. Nothing — the steel door was immovable.

The sudden heightening of senses, the pungent smell of cement and rain.

Footsteps clanged on the black iron of the fire escape. Johnny turned toward the stairwell — climb to the roof, maybe crawl up somehow. He took two steps, curling over the railing.

They were already in range.

He heard a popping sound from below, and his ribcage shuddered. And again. He tried to breathe past the pain lancing his chest. Chinese voices, and another voice, unidentifiable. Cold on his cheek, and he knew he was down on the ironwork. Something like boiling soup poured on his stomach. He felt some leathery thing brush his face, and then a whooshing of wings peeling away across a vast black canyon.

Chapter 2

Ray Infantino strode along the red brick sidewalks of Beacon Hill in Boston. Old elms shaded the stately row houses, set close to the narrow streets and bordered with iron gates and granite steps. Small gardens exploded with color—foxglove, bleeding heart, purple cone flowers spilling over the brick. Across the street, a group of tourists fired madly away with their cameras at a particularly well-preserved brick mansion. One of those lush days in a fast and furious New England summer—it made the existence of winter seem an impossibility.

For the upcoming meeting, Ray dressed in a navy blue suit with a cobalt shirt and patterned gold tie. He avoided button-down collars, a sign of epic repression.

He knew that he would be scrutinized by one of Boston's best criminal defense lawyers, Lucas Michaels. Lucas had invited him to his home office, where he was working for the day. Lawyers like Lucas often had ambivalent relationships with investigators. Investigators could be a problem. They needed to be roped in all too often. Too many cowboys telling war stories from back in the day when their cocks got stiff without help from a little blue pill.

Ray rang at the door of a three-story Victorian row house topped with a copper dome that had faded to a green patina. The golden dome of the state house peeked over the hill a few blocks away. He brushed back a wave of unruly black hair, and pulled the suit jacket over his spare boxer's physique.

He rang again and heard a buzzing sound. The door clicked open, and Ray stepped into a foyer painted a brilliant white. A thin man in his sixties walked toward him.

"Lucas Michaels," the man said, extending his hand. "Thanks for coming over so soon, Ray." Lucas wore a faded blue polo shirt over tan slacks. His face was all sharp angles, topped by a crisply cut hedge of white hair. He looked fit and rested.

Although lawyers were often guilty for lauding each other with bloated reviews, Lucas's reputation as one of the top defense lawyers in the city was legitimate. His fame had not come easily. After working on the West Coast as a young lawyer, he had returned home to Boston and worked unheralded for many years as court–appointed counsel for indigent defendants. In 1963, he undertook the defense of the Scollay Slasher in a murder trial with national coverage. The defendant had murdered seven women in back alleys of the decaying Scollay Square section of Boston. He was acquitted after Lucas's brutal cross-examination of two witnesses exposed major flaws in the police investigation. He had never looked back, regularly defending the city's most hated and controversial figures. His reputation grew, one of thoroughness, a solid, if unspectacular, intelligence. And a certain ruthlessness. He seemed to enjoy eviscerating witnesses on the witness stand, even those he did not suspect were lying; he enjoyed it just a bit more than even the bruising standards of his profession allowed. "A feared elder statesman of the Boston defense bar," a mutual friend, Paul Artemis, had said of Lucas before arranging the meeting with Ray. "A real prick."

Ray knew that elder statesmen of the bar were often late payers. He'd make certain to get a retainer.

Lucas led Ray through the living room filled with dark, ornate furniture, and into an informal brick-walled study. Books of literature and law lined the walls. A white oak bar filled one side of the study. The two men sat down in overstuffed leather chairs. The smell of cigar smoke filled the air.

"I've heard a lot about you over the years," Lucas said. "Paul Artemis at Boswell & Giles spoke well of you. Said you were an uncommon talent."

Ray nodded in recognition of Artemis's name. "We did some work together on a civil rights case against the White

Aryan Nation."

"Paul said you have a talent for finding and handling witnesses. This might be the right case for that talent."

Ray tried to think of which investigator Lucas had worked with on past cases, but he drew a blank.

"Tell me more of your background," Lucas said. "How did you come to work in the PI field?"

"While in law school, I started working one summer for the Southern Law Project as an investigator," said Ray. "I developed a strategy for placing undercover operatives in hate groups. Based on some of the evidence we developed, the Law Center filed a civil RICO case and was able to seize the Aryan Knights' assets. Even the Aryan Knights name was turned over. They can't use the name anymore without infringing a trademark."

Lucas nodded. "That must have infuriated them. Sounds interesting. Those are some rough people."

"Rough," agreed Ray, fading out and thinking of the Project. He forced himself to think of the meeting, letting his thoughts of the Project diffuse in the air. *Ignore it.* "A few years later, I went out on my own. I specialize in interviewing witnesses, handling the fact-finding on complex cases," he concluded.

"Well, I hope you can assist me," Lucas said. "I have a client with a personal issue involving a young member of the family." Lucas stood up, walked behind the bar, and bent down to open a small refrigerator. "Can I get you something to drink?"

"Water is fine, thanks." Lucas returned with two miniature bottles of water, some fancy imported stuff with a label crowing about gelid springs and eternal life. Ray sipped his water, and waited.

Lucas shifted in his seat and made himself comfortable. "The client is a Chinese family who I have represented for many years in business matters. They are based in Hong Kong. They asked me to assist in locating a missing family member, a woman named Tania Kong. Her sister is the one who is leading this inquiry."

"Tania is of Chinese-Thai descent. She was always the black sheep of the family. She had a difficult childhood. Her natural mother died when she was a young child. Her father remarried a few years later. That unfortunate series of events brings us here."

Lucas paused and sipped his water. "Growing up, Tania was rebellious, depressed. She never got along with her stepmother." He shrugged and opened his hands. "The usual fairy tale. Tania was raised by her father in Hong Kong. The family fell on rough times when he passed away after being fatally injured in an auto accident. Tania was devastated by her father's death. As I said, her relationship with her stepmother was never warm. At age eighteen, she left the family compound and was living on her own."

Ray noticed that Lucas spoke in a formal, literary manner that, while probably appealing in court, could be off-putting in casual conversation. He was surprised by this habit, given Lucas dealt with criminal dregs. He forced himself to focus.

"A few years ago, after moving to San Francisco, she disappeared," said Lucas. He sat back in his chair. "The client is only now pursuing this. They tried to reach her every now and then, but she seems to have just dropped off the face of the earth."

"Does the family know of any friends in California?" asked Ray.

"None that we know. We have no address, no telephone number. This is why I called you. There is very little to go on. Nothing really." He leaned forward. "Do you think you can assist in finding her?"

"Absolutely. There are things that can be done, local city records, courts, that type of thing. Interviews with people—"

Lucas interrupted, "That brings me to the next point: the client is a prominent family in Hong Kong. Various businesses, restaurants, nightclubs. Real estate on both U.S.

coasts. They don't want to be on page one with a story about their wayward little girl. That is a major concern. Avoid the paparazzi. They simply want to find her and make sure she is all right."

"I understand. Do you have a photo of Tania?"

"Not yet, but I will have the client provide one. The photos will be a bit dated, obviously."

"And you say the family does not have even a last known address in the city?" asked Ray. "Maybe I can speak with the family just to confirm that they have no information."

"Certainly," Lucas said. "The client has told me they have no information about where she may have lived in San Francisco. She never corresponded with them while she was there. Not by mail or telephone. She was reclusive."

"So there really is not much to go on."

"Not much at all."

Ray nodded, rubbed his chin. Find the missing girl. Easy enough, usually.

"I know you cannot give guarantees," continued Lucas, "but approximately how long do you think before you can begin to see some results?"

"I would give it at least a few weeks, but can't be certain at this point," Ray replied. "I'll run her name and date of birth just to see if something obvious pops up in the databases. Although I doubt that, based on what you said about a previous investigator not finding her. I can be in San Francisco by Tuesday. This will probably require some lengthy public records research there. I'll need a retainer before I travel."

"That will not be an issue. What are your fees?"

"$195.00 per hour. Plus expenses."

"You charge more than most investigators," said Lucas.

"I get results. Usually anyway. This is a humbling business. I stay in good hotels, nothing ridiculous though. Travel time is billed; half this job is waiting for the golden moment."

"I understand," Lucas said, nodding. "I've taken clients to court to show them why I had to sit in a hallway while a judge conducts a motions hearing. But your fees will not be a problem. The client wants your best efforts and they expect to pay for it."

"I'll send over an engagement letter," said Ray. "I think a $10,000 retainer should be fine to start."

Ray handed Lucas a card. "I'll wait to see the photo before I make any plans. As I mentioned, any personal identifiers such as a date of birth or even a green card number, that would be helpful too."

"Yes, thanks for reminding me. I'll check on both points."

Lucas sat down at an antique desk in a corner of the room, where he jotted down some notes. Ray admired the oak wainscoting, honey colored and smooth. Lucas finished writing and stood up. He reached out his hand to Ray. "This client expects superior results. They always do. And that is why I called you. This type of case is probably routine for you."

Ray nodded. "It's routine — until it's not." He smiled. It was tempting, but he wasn't about to promise anything. Lucas stared at him for a moment, and then a tight smile crossed his face. "I look forward to working with you," he said. The men shook hands, and Ray walked toward the door.

Ray walked down the granite stairs and headed toward Beacon Street. He cut through the Public Gardens. Stands of willows arched over the swan boats as college kids paddled languidly through the dark green water. He strolled past expensive bistros and shops on Newbury Street, and walked into the brassy dusk of the Capitol Grill steakhouse. The show was on: the glasses sparkled, the bartender mixed drinks in a lunchtime fury, a busty waitress let select customers look down her blouse a little bit. He sat down in a window seat and ordered a rare steak with French fries.

The meal came and Ray dug into the steak. He would have to thank Paul Artemis for referring him to Lucas. Personal recommendations were the touchstone on which the private world of lawyers relied. It would be a good case — defined as a riddle wrapped in a puzzle situated in an interesting locale. And backed with a sufficient budget. And while he was in California, he would personally undertake work on the Project, perform the necessary pruning. It was long overdue. This would be his first trip to the city in five years.

Ray delved into the delicious rare slab of beef and watched the antics of the lunch crowd. Then he paid the bill and headed back to work.

* * *

Lucas watched as Ray headed down the street. He had not expected a cowboy, and he was pleased. He had heard a story from a colleague about this man. The trial lawyer had asked Infantino on the witness stand what he did for a living; Infantino had replied that he looked into people's eyes to tell if they were lying. Laughs all around, and the jury loved it. Lucas suspected Infantino was only partly joking. Lucas knew what his client wanted: someone who had yet to rot in the suburbs, someone not easily denied. This was the guy.

He called California from a disposable phone he used for three months and then tossed. The line was picked up.

"Our investigator will be out there next week."

"Who is he?

"Ray Infantino. Highly recommended for this sort of matter. Once he finishes his work, make sure you finish yours."

JOHN F. NARDIZZI

Chapter 3

A t Hunan House Restaurant in San Francisco's Chinatown, Tamo sat back in his chair. The forty year old Shanghai native had a crude bulk that made other men step back despite his lack of height. An assortment of scars and cuts on his hands and neck were living mementos of a highly evolved violent streak. Tamo finished the last call and jammed the cell phone in his pocket. Damn thing was overheating. He picked at his dinner of spicy shrimp.

The message came two hours before, and it was very clear: The bosses wanted the whore. And they wanted her now. She was a witness who saw something downtown and got out of the building before the job was done. Cops had picked her up, interviewed her. They couldn't take any chances.

He filtered a slightly different version into the flinty night. The long reach of the Black Fist Triad came into play: photos passed, descriptions detailed, names and addresses reviewed. Kids selling newspapers on Kearny, the night clerk at the liquor store, bartenders, club kids, truck drivers, anyone of them could make an easy grand for a positive ID on the girl. She had taken something—speculation was money, but no one was certain—taken something that was not hers to take. That was the story. No one asked whose money, and no one asked how much. People seemed sensitive to the vibration. The Triad was calling for justice for one of their own. When a tiger gets angry, the grass gets trampled. No one wanted to be the grass.

Tamo now had over seventy men sitting on her apartment. The young bloods loved stakeouts. This was the private eye shit they saw in the movies. How good some of the kids were at surveillance, though, was open for evaluation. But what some of them lacked in experience, they made up in sheer numbers—that was why he had fourteen cars out there. The men parked at staggered points around the block. Four or five guys to a car, meandering around the neighborhood.

He had three cars on Larkin Street, which had sunk into its customary vileness by 11:00 PM. Solitary men in hoodies dealt meth in the shadows of withered trees dying on the sidewalk. Suburban addicts drove around the block, nervous but desperate, risking it all for a one hour high. Tranny hookers perched on street corners. A steady trail of cars rolled by with young guys ogling the tits and ass. A few Triad soldiers razzed a Latina tranny in red heels with enormous fake breasts bursting through her blouse. "Ass-smellin' bitches!" she hissed. Billy didn't take that shit from no man in a dress. He tried to get out of the back seat to bash her skull. The crew held him back, laughing crazily, high fives all around. The tranny stalked up Post Street. The men returned to watching the apartment.

Tamo left the restaurant and had a beer at an underground card game near Stockton. So many tunnels had been dug in the basement that no one was sure anymore which building they were sitting beneath. By 1:00 AM, he was thoroughly pissed at the lack of news. He worked the cell again. He ordered dozens more soldiers into the Tenderloin, North Beach and Telegraph Hill, the bars near the Marina, downtown, SOMA, the Mission. The soldiers walked all night long, a scanned photo from some years back jammed in a pocket; others sat in cars watching the clubs empty out and compared faces to a photo set on the dashboard. Not perfect, but better than nothing. They scoured Chinatown and Nob Hill, driving slowly and ripping the streets with eyeballs. They drove up and down Broadway staring at any girl who fit the profile: Chinese, early 20s, pretty eyes, face as seen in the picture.

No sign of Tania by the next morning. Another hour. No word by noon. Tamo smacked the table—how the hell do six hundred men not find this girl walking the streets? He made more phone calls, burning through the anger with sheer activity.

"Get everyone out there. Roll out every dickweed by the carload!" All they wanted was one little whore.

Chapter 4

The sun was shining and joggers crowded the crumbling paths on the banks of the Charles River. Ray headed to his office in Cambridge, located on the top floor of a 18th century brick building near Harvard Square. Harvard College had been founded in 1756,the nation's first men's college. As the college's elite reputation spread, the neighborhood outside its red brick walls grew with it. Some people thought the neighborhood had grown too much and lost its distinct flavor; it now resembled any other urban center. Ray strode past the few funky cafes and bookstores that refused to be shouldered aside as national retailers moved in, undaunted by rising rents. A crew of young punks at the subway station kept a wary eye on the upward mobility of the Square.

Ray walked into his office. Bookcases lined the crimson walls. A Fiji mask hung near the door, grinning a razor smile, a crazed god watching over some forgotten crevice of the universe. His receptionist and editor, Sheri Haynes, sat at her desk in a sunny corner.

"Good morning," he said.

"Hello Ray." She stopped editing a report and looked up. "Nice shirt. Love that color."

"A question for you. The guy at Brooks said this color is mauve." He pulled at his shirt. "I say lavender."

"It's lavender, Ray. He's color blind."

"We agree on something." Ray poured a cup of black coffee, and sat down.

"That attorney overnighted the retainer," said Sheri. "For the case in California."

Glancing out the window at the street, Ray saw a man wearing a T-shirt, shorts, and sneakers with black dress socks cross Massachusetts Avenue. The man, probably a professor, soon disappeared behind the brick wall of Harvard Yard. Ray shook his head in disgust—denizens of Harvard had a polluted sense of style.

He turned to a tidy pile of mail on his desk and opened a letter from Lucas Michaels. It contained a check written out for ten thousand dollars and two photos of Tania. A brief note listed Tania's date of birth and Social Security Number.

He looked closely at the photos. One was a close-up of an Asian woman with long black hair combed back and parted in the middle. Her skin was tan, darker than most Chinese, leavened as it was with Thai blood. Her eyes were set just a bit too close, so that she was bumped from the ranks of the beautiful into the merely intriguing— a far better category, in Ray's opinion. Her face radiated an inquisitive intelligence. The second photo showed her thoughtful, unsmiling, holding her awkward teenage body slightly toward the camera. She was dressed in jeans with a white shirt that just showed a sliver of stomach. A note stated that the first photo was taken when Tania was twenty years old, while the second was taken when Tania was seventeen years old.

Ray turned to his computer and ran Tania's name and birth date through several locator databases. The databases were built on information from credit applications, phone records, real estate transactions, licensing records— the citizenry of the United States reduced to its essential numbers and sequences. Tania did not come up in any database. Ray guessed that she was using cash, flying low to avoid the radar.

He looked down at his calendar, checking the schedule. No pressing meetings for the next few days. He worked mostly for lawyers, narrowly intelligent men who still wore suits on Fridays and tried to look older than they were. Serious faces for serious business. On their behalf he undertook the messy work of facts, of witnesses with criminal convictions and flawed memories. The thousand nicks and scars that make a human.

They asked him to interview witnesses. They asked him

to put people under surveillance. He had a modest army of surveillance operatives. Rich clients especially loved that aspect of investigations: a transitory omnipresence, watching your opponent's daily rituals. They called on weekends, demanding constant updates. They wanted descriptions, auto makes, shoe sizes, and facial details. They wanted the name of the awesome blond. He once had a client in California who had requested that Ray keep an enemy under surveillance around the clock for two years. There was a beauty to such demented pursuits.

He decided he would waste no more time in Boston. His personality was geared to projects, numbered lists. Check them off and the day is done. He devoted time to it, the detailed tasks in a notebook, the required follow-up. And now he had two projects in California.

"Sheri, will you take this to the bank now?" He handed her the check. "I'm heading west."

"You're off where?" she asked, coming to him and taking the check.

"San Francisco."

Sheri stared at him. "Are you working on Cherry yourself?"

"Partly," said Ray. "The check covers other work actually."

She paused, an odd look on her face. "You ready to jump back into that?"

"San Francisco is where I have to go. The path to a molten ending is made of a thousand cold steps."

Sheri adjusted her glasses. "What's that from? Faulkner?"

"That's from me," said Ray. Then he flicked on the computer and booked a flight to San Francisco.

Chapter 5

Head low, Tania skittered through the narrow, sun-blasted alley. It looked too open, a concrete shooting gallery. This place always made her nervous. But she had to get off Market Street. The wind ripped down from Twin Peaks, blowing newspapers against her leg.

She pulled her hoodie close to her face. She looked like a homeless wreck, a huge ratty sweatshirt, old sneakers. She should cut off her long hair—too noticeable.

Her friend lived in a gray house with a heavy steel door. She looked toward Mission and back to Market. No one was following. She took the key, opened the door and slipped inside. The door clanged shut behind her and she breathed out audibly.

In the hours after the murder, she had been out of her mind with fear. She had left the hotel running but a cop stopped her after he saw her leaving the front gate. She sat in the car, and he took her downtown. As the cruiser pulled away, they were watching, three of them, staring at her through the glass. She told the cops nothing and got out few hours later, but the damage was done. She had survived the shooting and now they thought she was a snitch. A death sentence two times over.

They would shoot her ten, twenty times, right in the neck and face. The girls called these kids the walking dead, because despite their youth, they harbored no hope, no feelings. The whole thing involved a different breed now, these kids, they planned nothing and just reacted, cyclone spasms of mayhem. Pulled from typhoid slums in China, they only wanted to live large for a few crazed years and then die like men. The triad promised them a life where both desires would be fulfilled.

She had eaten almost nothing for days. She would shape shift and let hunger carve her appearance into something new, unrecognizable. She couldn't eat anyway. Every goddamn guy that came near her. . . .

She remembered one story of a triad member who shot a guy from a motorcycle. He wasn't sure if his mission was complete. That was the word the kids used used—they went on missions. The guy stopped a motor bike in front of a crowd of people. Revved the engine and sent smoke into the crowd. Then he walked over to the kid lying on the street, bent down, and emptied the gun into his face. This was who they were sending after her.

The night the men had stormed the hotel, two of them charging up the fire escape, they put a dozen bullets in her friend's back. Jesus, the way one guy came in, calmly, methodically, like he was coming to fix the sink. Then he just unloaded everything at Cindy, the booming shots in the hallway, total chaos.

She panicked and ran for her life. The sight of a girl running down the street half-naked did not arouse undue suspicion in San Francisco. She made it into some night club, just to get off the street. She had no money—Johnny got shot before he paid her. The club turned out to be some sort of S&M club. There were different floors with chains drilled into the walls and wood contraptions that looked like torture devices from a distant Spanish century. The lighting was dim, red, surreal. Smells of cigarette smoke, sweaty bodies, a desperate kind of lust in the air. Tomorrow, no one would remember she had been here; this was a place that erased memories.

She walked through the cavernous club for the entire night, just killing time. At 4:30 AM, the place was dying down a bit. She found a huge hole in a wall, some abandoned expansion project, downstairs in the basement. She slipped inside and cried herself to sleep. The club closed and no one bothered her.

She woke up the next day, and slipped out the rear door while a beer truck unloaded. She was starving. Her teeth felt nasty. She needed a shower.

She stopped by a store on the corner of Mission. Inside the grocery, an Asian kid alternated between reading a magazine and staring at her. Too long, she thought. Heart hammering her ribs. She paid for a candy bar and an iced tea, then walked outside, half-expecting the last view of her life would be the battered yellow doorjamb of this little store.

Her foot hit the pavement. The second she was clear of the door, she started running.

JOHN F. NARDIZZI

Chapter 6

Ray chatted with an Ohio housewife sitting next to him on the plane. "That must be interesting," she remarked upon learning he was an investigator. Everyone said that. Sometimes, sometimes not. Ray didn't want to repeat any war stories, and grew quiet after the pretzels arrived. He watched the tiny houses below as the plane began its slow descent into San Francisco International Airport. Red salt ponds lined the coast to the south, while the city of San Francisco lay to the north.

San Francisco, California. Where you went when no one on the East Coast was talking to you anymore. You traversed the country on a personal gold rush to show parents, childhood tormentors—everyone you ever knew— that something rare boiled inside you. An accident of geography lifted San Francisco into the ranks of sublimely beautiful cities. Sharply etched hills—Telegraph Hill, Russian Hill, Nob Hill—offered sudden vistas of the blue Pacific, which drew the day to a close with a foggy gray curtain. San Francisco was rich, seductive, insatiable, demanding, and even after you saw her grimy face and wasted ways, you loved her like a woman—the endless promise of California.

Ray expected to interview numerous people over the next few days. He had rented Detroit spawn. A Cadillac: big, American, faintly ridiculous. He liked pulling up to witnesses in a Caddy. Americans had been raised on mob movies, and instinctively associated the Caddy with power, ruin, conspiratorial afternoons in villa gardens. Something like that.

After clearing the airport, Ray headed up Highway 280, taking signs for the Port of San Francisco. The traffic flowed and weaved as he arrived at 6th Street. He headed east toward the waterfront. He arrived at the Embarcadero, where palm trees graced the median and a pale strip of glass brick lined the sidewalk. The Bay Bridge soared over the bay, straddling the twin cities of Oakland and San Francisco.

He turned right on Broadway, racing past the strip joints and restaurants, zigzagged his way on the small side street just before the tunnel, then left on Mason over Nob Hill. It felt good remembering all the old shortcuts. Ray parked and walked a few blocks to pick up a cheese steak sandwich. Then he headed toward the criminal courts. He had decided he would check the dockets first to see if Tania had caught a case.

In every county seat in the United States, a vast public record exists in the form of court cases, all indexed by last name. On the civil side, the records contain a history of the grievances, complaints and assorted ailments that plagued a society. And on the criminal side, courts maintain historical dockets of deviance and sick behavior, a blueprint of the lives of society's incorrigibles.

Ray was dressed for court in dress pants, a dark blue shirt with a tan jacket. He drove South of Market to the Hall of Justice. Nine stories tall, and built like a bomb shelter, it was nerve center of law enforcement in the city of San Francisco. He walked through the metal detector, strolling past predators prowling the tiled hallways: rapists, murderers, district attorneys. The tiles made it easy to scrub off the accumulated filth. The rough banter of probation officers, lead-eyed felons, and thick-handed cops. The veteran cops and criminals had an easy familiarity with the place, comfortable in each other's presence. They understood that they needed each other. They had spent time together in the past, and would likely do so again.

For others, fear and rage clung palpably to the walls here, lives determined in small courtrooms with swinging doors. Signs in English and Spanish on the wall:

Do Not Chew Gum In Court. Weapons Are Not Allowed In The Courtroom.

Conversations boomed and echoed in the hallway so that privacy was something you left at home, for other buildings, other times, a luxury the rich enjoyed in carpeted homes with solid wood doors. An odd sense of racial peace reigned, for this was a place for the democratic poor — black, white, brown, it didn't matter. One look around confirmed that the jaws of justice chewed meat in all flavors.

Ray walked over to a clerk at the service desk, an attractive Latina in her forties. She was entombed in a bulletproof glass cubicle. He had to shout through a narrow slit to make himself understood. The clerk had dark eyes, and a bosom barely constrained in a light green suit. She got away with it; her curvy nerve got her through.

"Can I help you?" she asked.

"I'd like to check a name for any cases going back to the 1980's." He jotted down Tania's name and birth date on a sheet of paper.

The clerk checked the alphabetized index on her computer for Kong and printed out the results: one case from 1997. Ray filled out an order form and requested the case file. The clerk disappeared behind some rolling file cabinets. After a few minutes, she returned with the file.

"I like your jacket," said Ray.

"Thanks," the clerk handed him the file, smiling. "No fear of a full color palette."

She laughed. "I like to spice it up in here." She rapped the Plexiglas with her knuckles. "Place is decorated like a penitentiary." She handed him the file. "Here you go. Let me know if you need copies," she said.

He was feeling better already. Funny how a bit of human interaction could mean so much to a traveler. He opened the case file, but saw only a single sheet of paper, the criminal complaint. It contained the barest amount of information, announcing with the quaintly Communist language used by California courts: *People of California v. Tania Kong*. The charge was California Penal Code Section 315: Tania had been arrested for working at a house of prostitution.

There was nothing else in the case — no photos or affidavits or legal papers. The briefly worded complaint stated that on May 24, 1997, Tania Kong had been arrested for prostitution after police raided a brothel at 781 Jackson Street in Chinatown. No other defendants were named.

Ray jotted down the address, and copied the complaint. He returned the file to the light green lovely in her glass cube.

"What did this one do?" she asked.

"A rapscallion. Hardcore."

The clerk glanced at the complaint. "Poor girl had some bad love."

"That's one way to look at it."

Ray thanked the clerk and left the courthouse.

Chapter 7

Four muscular Asian men strutted along the Embarcadero, radiating that odd mix of intimidation and restraint peculiar to Asian gangs. The men had spent a lot of hours building muscle; being young and violent, they showed off the results of their work with the iron. Thick trapezes danced beneath the muscle tees, hard chests thrust out, triceps rippling. But the men gave way to tourists, didn't try to overdo the turf walk. They were on business, simple and direct: hunt down Tania Kong.

They walked past an outside cafe, scanning the people. Fit men in black spandex and funny-looking helmets straddled titanium bikes, or lounged on the grass. Kids walked by with their parents, munching on junk food.

They had been looking for Tania for six days. No sign of her anywhere. Everyone had been sure it would be over in forty-eight hours. But they were wrong. Excitement leaked away; frustration set in.

Ricky flicked a cigarette to the sidewalk as he reconnoitered the perimeter of the cafe. "I once seen this show about missing persons—you don't find them in twenty-four hours, you be fucked."

Dan looked at him. "Ahh shut ya' cake hole." The other guys glared at Ricky, resenting the implication. The fuck-up was reaching major proportions. Word filtered down from the bosses—they were pissed. Tamo was riding them hard. A subliminal pressure was building, the guys could feel it, like the tipping point in football when a linebacker crunches into a quarterback to jar the ball loose. A spirit of collision. Someone had to make something happen soon.

Last night at Buddha Bar, Xio "Kenny" Chu came up with an idea. Lean, well-dressed, a smooth talker, Kenny was dating a girl who worked at a hospital and drove a van for elderly people. He told the crew that the van had "Elderly Services" printed in blue block letters on the side and was outfitted with stuff for the oldsters—the van actually tilted down and had a little conveyor belt that lifted the old people out the door.

Well, the great thing is, my girl takes the van home each night, she got the keys." He smiled broadly over his beer as he told everyone. "We can do missions from the handicap van. Roomy and they don't attract a lot of suspicion."

He met her at a club, and they did the club hookup, sleeping together after one night out and then trying to salvage the thing and get to know each other afterward. He was still banging her on occasion.

"She told me that if I needed wheels, I could take the van anytime I need it."

So now the crew had the handicap wheels for the day, cruising around and hunting Tania from the van. They could park in handicap spots — anywhere really — because elderly people voted, they had all kinds of rights, and who was going to ask a van used to help elderly people to move anyway?

So they piled inside and roamed the city. It was funny shit, the van cruising heavily, the way the door opened and the van tilted down like a decrepit elephant so the oldsters could step on.

The guys carried six guns on board, four pistols and two sawed off shotguns. Kenny and Dan placed one shotgun in each corner of the van so they could cover all angles, a rolling fortress. The guns had homemade silencers on them, thick as cans and stuffed with sound deadening fiberglass.

After a dull morning, they parked at the water looking over the East Bay. Kenny and Sammy got off to pick up some lunch when they saw her sitting in the cafe. Asian girl, petite, eyes with a certain Western look to them. Right height, right profile. They ran back to the van to check the picture.

"Yep, it's Tania," said Kenny. They passed the picture back and forth, and voted. Sammy shook his head no. They argued. "I'm just saying, the girl in the cafe looks different. I don't think it's her." But Dan, squat and eager, muttered, "Let's do this." The mission just seemed inevitable. No one listened to that douche bag Sammy anyway.

Dan pointed to the driver seat. Kenny hustled up to the front and pulled away. They had found their target, they felt the pressure. Plus, Kenny had told them his girlfriend had to drive the van to work the next day.

The van cruised down the Embarcadero toward the cafe. The shooters crouched near the shaded windows. They stopped for a few minutes until Tania got up and left the cafe. She sipped a coffee as she strolled in front of one of docks on the marina. The van rolled slowly by. A rear window cracked open. Dan unloaded, sending a muffled blast right at Tania. Her right shoulder evaporated in a red mist. She toppled over. Then another shot and another shot, muffled humps, as the van rolled peaceably by. Tania lay still on the concrete. There was some ricochet action and a biker toppled over, crashing into a cafe table.

"Hit a mushroom, hahahah!" Kenny loved the mayhem. The shared adrenaline rush, four hard, young badasses. The guys were laughing and belting each other, they should have videotaped the bitch and put it up on Youtube. The geek on the mountain bike was just a bonus.

People on the sidewalk were looking around now, a girl down, a biker screaming. They scanned the street and over the water and looked down the Embarcadero. The elderly van lumbered along, innocuous and overlooked.

Later the papers came out with the story and the girl's name. Melissa. She was from out of town, a student from Wisconsin.

Another mistake. The bosses were not happy. Dan, Ricky, Sammy and Kenny got the call. A dark SUV came by their Clement Street apartment and drove them to a private bar on Grant Street. Some heavy hitters there, soldiers from the top crews. Tamo had warned that bullshit mistakes would not be tolerated. Two of the soldiers dragged Kenny down a stairwell to the basement. Kenny resisted a bit. One of the men snapped the butt of his handgun on his skull, a hard thwack. Kenny's limbs jerked a crazy dance. They shoved the other guys downstairs and tossed Kenny into a shallow pit dug into the floor filled with filthy water. Beer cans and cigarette butts floated on the surface. One of the men opened Kenny's skull with a pipe. Blood mixed with the dark waters. Head wounds always looked worse than they were, the pressure of veins on the skull shot the blood everywhere, but still, the moaning from Kenny unnerved his friends.

Dan, Sammy, and Ricky got knocked around a bit before Tamo decided they had enough. Kenny lay unconscious in front of the others, bleeding into the half dug pit. They emerged with shocked looks from the basement into a side alley. Something different in their faces now. They blinked in the summer light and eyeballed the dumpsters. Still worried the beat down was not over.

Tamo watched them in silence. Then laughter geysered up through him so rapidly that he rocked back and forth, almost dancing. He loved this life. When you felt part of something so close to the top, it was close to perfection. Like a ruined god.

"Dumb little fuckers. We like the handicap van though. Smart!" Tamo pointed to his skull. "That's why you're still alive."

A joke went around the Triad, the crews needed to increase their missionary work: seduce more girls who worked at hospitals, nursing homes, schools for the blind.

Chapter 8

Ray walked the trash-strewn streets of the Civic Center back to his car. He parked on Sutter Street and checked into the Commodore Hotel, a Jazz-era hotel known for its informal style on the Tenderloin outskirts. He had good memories of the place, having done some spoken word performances here a few times with a blues band. He popped into the hotel bar, decorated completely in red, with one wall comprised entirely of champagne glasses encased in bulletproof glass.

He checked his phone for Dominique's number. He knew he could save time finding archived case files by making inquiries with the San Francisco Police Department. And that meant reaching out to Dominique. He was not sure he wanted to call her just yet, and had thought he might resist for longer than one day. Well, he decided, he had as legitimate an excuse as he could have asked. He punched her number on his cell.

At 7:00 PM. Ray walked over Nob Hill, watching the sun sink and stain the sky a purple-blue patina. A cable car clanked up the hill, arms of tourists jutting and pointing at the stately homes. On his right, La Dolce Vita, an Italian bistro where he had eaten dozens of times with Diana. The life he had lived. A black fury threatened to swamp his senses. He shook off thoughts of the past and entered the restaurant.

The noise level was deafening. A row of impossibly good-looking people sat at the bar, waiting for their tables. Ray sat at the section near the window that looked over Hyde Street. He would watch for the crescendo of craning necks that he knew would follow Dominique Arnello into the restaurant. It was more than a trophy exhibition. Her impeccable bearing elevated walking into a moving art. The artistry of the banal, one of the keys to living.

While studying law at the University of California,

Dominique's friendship redeemed the drab social life that plagues most first year law students. Starting law school at age forty one, she was older than most of her classmates. Her high-voltage intellect and sleek figure comprised an unusual combination of gifts, and for that, many of her classmates could never forgive her. She refused to look the part often assumed by young female law students: either the devout, unsleeping scholar of law, or the sharp-tempered courtroom medusa with swords sticking out of her hair. She was just Dominique, kind, intelligent, and seemingly there for the sheer joy of it.

Dominique arrived at the restaurant a few minutes later, black curly hair down to her shoulders, a lavender business suit with a strategic amount of cleavage, showing to great effect, a string of pearls. The wave of heads rolled as expected.

Ray took in the sight of the woman he had once known so intimately — olive skin, deep eyes the color of fallen oak leaves. He thought she looked unbelievably healthy, radiant as a newly fired sun.

She saw him right away and cut through the crowd. He reached out and they embraced. They looked at each other, so much to say. The host guided them to a table. They ordered a bottle of Cabernet. Both flush with muted excitement, talking in that tender way when people meet for the first time in years. The wine came and they relaxed.

"Do you keep in touch with any of the old crew?"

"I hardly see anyone. Once in awhile I see Patrick in court. Remember him?"

"He was the guy who tore pages out of the first year assignments."

"You remember that!" she laughed. "He always denied it."

"Not convincingly," said Ray.

The noise level in the dining room was rising as wine glasses were drained.

"Didn't you two shoot pool all through the first year?"

"If you are referring to my billiards sessions, I can only say the time spent was exaggerated. Pool relaxed me." Ray took a drink. "That, among other things."

Dominique looked at him and smiled. The waiter brought some sourdough bread.

"What are you working on these days?"

"The usual," said Dominique. "Some overcharged drug cases. Black teenagers from Oakland getting maxed out in federal court. And the kingpin, some white dude, free in the suburbs somewhere." She sipped her wine. "So what brings you to California?"

Ray told her about Lucas Michaels and his efforts in locating a missing girl. "She slipped beneath the radar looking for her California dream."

"Let me know if I can help. If you need office space. "

"I will. Thanks."

"Any leads?" Dominique asked.

"A big one surfaced today. Municipal Court handled a case where she was charged with prostitution a few years ago. But there was hardly any paperwork in the case file. What's the retention policy on misdemeanors?"

"The clerk's office is getting rid of a lot of old files. Clogging up the old courthouse. There's no place left for the stuff."

"Any suggestions on how to get more background on that arrest?"

"A vice detective I know might be able to help you. Waymon Pierce. He'd be a great place to start."

"Good."

"He's an odd bird, a real talker. But he's seen it all. I'll call him tomorrow for you."

The waitress, a skinny gruff woman, came and took their orders. Ray was surprised that she had elbowed her way into the hospitality business. He ordered swordfish, while Dominique ordered tortellini with cream sauce.

"Glad you didn't just order a salad. I hate it when women do that."

"Me? Please. Plus, you're paying." She paused. "I am glad that you called. It seemed like geography got in the way of our friendship."

"Despite everything we said."

"By the way, how's your family, your mother and father? I loved your father, with those shirts!"

"They're doing fine. Living in Boston still. I see them every week."

She paused and looked at the floor. "Ray, I'm sorry about what happened to your fiancé. That was terrible."

Ray looked at her. "Thanks."

I read about it. I wanted to call. But I felt . . . I don't know."

"It's OK. I didn't answer the phone for a year."

"But I should have done something," she said, her brow furrowing. "That was wrong."

"It's OK. Really. It's tough to talk about. Even now."

They sat awkwardly, waiting for the food. The host was making a big show of seating a well-dressed older couple, who ate up the attention.

"How is the investigation going?" Dominique asked. "They indict anyone?"

"They never did. We think the bombing was retaliation for my work with the Law Center a few years back. We developed evidence that an Aryan Knights group planned the murders of several Mexican migrant workers found bludgeoned to death in camps near the border."

"And they tied all this to you?"

"The group knew my face. But privacy is not what it once was. All those goddamn internet sites selling personal data," he said, trailing off. "Somehow, they tracked me here." Ray sipped his wine and took a deep breath to calm himself.

"Who is the main suspect?"

"Dude named Bobby Cherry. An investigator saw him on the Embarcadero the week before the bombing, spreading discomfort among the tourists." Ray fingered a knife. "Skinny white boy calling for a race war. The coming of the great white god."

"Did the police ever question him?" Dominique asked.

"He was interviewed. He admitted being present at the wharf, but denied heading into North Beach. Nothing could tie him in."

Ray looked around for the waiter and signaled for another drink. Dominique sat back, and frowned. She started to say something when the food arrived.

The restaurant grew noisy. Once Ray and Dominique had a few bites of dinner the gloom disappeared. The red wine loosened nuggets of conversation. They laughed about old times, lovingly chopping down friends who weren't at the table to defend themselves. They were in the early stages of an old dance resumed. Best taken slow.

"This swordfish is great—would have a food critic fingering the thesaurus," Ray said.

Dominique laughed. "I hate food critics. They're either hack authors or failed chefs. Not good enough for either."

They finished the meal. "Anything you need this week, just call," Dominique said.

"I will. I have something else going here. Some surveillance on another case. Recommend anyone?"

"There's a PI firm downtown I've used a couple of times. I'll call over and have them get in touch with you."

Wrapped in conversation, they finally noticed that the restaurant was emptying.

"This waitress looks like she wants to dive-bomb the table," Ray said. "She's ready to close out."

Ray paid the bill, the waitress muttering a thank-you in his direction as they moved to the door.

Lightly stewed in red wine, they ambled to the door, brushing arms as they walked into the night.

"It was great to see you."

"Yeah, great to see you too, Ray. I'm so glad you called."

"The past is the past," he said, not knowing what that meant.

"I have to go now."

"Another drink?"

"I really do have to go Ray," she said smiling. "Call me tomorrow. I don't trust you yet after midnight."

Ray stopped walking. "How about after two?"

"How about after sunrise," she replied. "We can talk then."

"Sunrise? You worried I'm a vampire?" He showed his teeth.

She ignored him, smiling at some private thought.

A cab slowed in front of the restaurant. Dominique got into the rear seat, a vision of lavender and exposed toes. Ray smiled, humming an old song. For the better, he thought. She was a beautiful person in every way. He realized just how much he missed her, the joy of life that radiated from her.

The cab pulled away. Ray walked on Hyde Street toward downtown as it descended to the outer reaches of the Tenderloin. Fog drifted across the hilltop and through the dark alleyways. He passed laundromats and bistros, a corner pizzeria with a jade plant overgrowing its windows. On Sutter Street, a pair of women perched on a street corner, garish birds trolling for crumbs. One in a red leather contraption that screamed hooker, the other dressed in a cocktail dress several sizes too small. Ray walked by, nodded. One of the women replied in a deep voice, a basso profundo. The juxtaposition of female curves and male audio jarred his senses. Still, he had to admit that the tranny looked better than the waitress at the restaurant.

Ray reached the hotel. The Red Room was pulsing with twenty year old men practicing elaborate approach rituals on anything resembling a female. A clueless fratboy wearing bowling shoes and a green sweatshirt tested a line — "Hey, nice cookies." A blond woman frowned, and looked for something to swing. Several men roared with laughter.

The spectral neon blue from the hotel sign leaked into his room. He didn't mind; he had kept Christmas lights up year round in his old apartment in law school. Sometimes he just liked to keep them lit, even in summer. He remembered

Dominique busting his ass about it once, like he was some old dago with lights lining the restaurant ceiling. He fell asleep instantly, nostalgic and exhausted.

Chapter 9

7:12 AM. Jet-lagged and sandy-eyed, Ray reached for the water glass on the night stand. He needed a drink; the antiseptic air of the hotel was irritating his lungs. He showered, scrubbing hard with the face cloth. The soap was wrapped in crisp paper and tied with a string. Smelled good, like lavender. He wondered if it worked any better than regular soap.

He dressed in a pair of olive slacks, a black jacket and black leather shoes. He took the stairs to a diner in the lobby and ordered the house special: thick French toast with home fries dusted with paprika. The place was a classic, with hard-ass waitresses busting chops as they brought carbo-overload to each table. Breakfast was the most unpretentious meal of the day.

The local paper was a horror, all ads and no news. Ray finished quickly. Then he paid the bill and went back to his room.

The message light on the phone was blinking. Dominique had called: the old cop, Waymon Pierce, was happy to help in any way he could. As he had recently retired from the force and apparently was not leaving home much, Ray could drop by anytime. That was always the case when Dominique brought those dark eyes to bear. Men rearranged things, cleared their schedules, purged themselves of crappy attitudes. Beauty may fade, but it packs a short-life wallop.

Ray jotted down Waymon's address, which was located in San Lorenzo, a suburb in the East Bay. He headed over to the garage and the valet had his car driven to the front. Ray turned right on to Sutter Street and made a series of right turns to Jones Street, heading into the Tenderloin.

In the 1930's, the Tenderloin had housed San Francisco's budding film industry. Many of the grand edifices remained intact, Victorian residences with quoins and cornices and carved wood statuary, silent testimony to the era of San Francisco's celluloid dreams.

The neighborhood had changed. Middle class families, black and white, had fled the city core for big green lawns and a TV in every room. Now, corner sidewalks were slick with piss and blood, and other human slime. Derelicts walked on Jones with their heads down, baseball-capped and anonymous. Homeless AIDS patients, the evidence of the thing all over their faces, red blotches, black ditches for eyes. A druggy violence pervaded whole blocks. Hawk-eyed young guns strutted past buildings jabbed with massage parlors and windowless lounges. The bars—when they had a name at all—sloughed off prosaic names: "Black Bottle," "Tipsy's," "The Driftwood," and "Thirsty Club". Bartenders revived broken men who muttered into their beer, bleary-eyed in the middle of the afternoon: bankrupts, felons, unemployed hit men, crack heads. This was the city's underbelly, crammed into a six-block dead zone. Only the children redeemed the place, laughing as they frolicked in fortified playgrounds under watchful eyes.

Waymon Pierce had patrolled the Tenderloin for over twenty years.

Ray arrived at the address he had been given for Waymon. A man wearing jeans and a neat white T-shirt stood in the doorway of a California bungalow fronted by neatly trimmed grass. Short of stature but with a hard lean body that belied his age, Waymon Pierce stepped outside as Ray approached. Waymon's face, however, reflected his age—it was a crisscross masterpiece of wrinkles and bony clefts.

"Hope I'm not intruding," said Ray.

"For a friend of Dominique's?" he shrugged.

"She's a good friend. We went to school together." He left out the law part.

"You have case work all the way here in California? You must be doing well for yourself."

"Things are good," Ray said. Waymon invited him inside. They stepped into a dark living room. It was a museum of 1970's decor: shag rugs, and a lumpy sofa, all dark brown, nature's safest color. A furry gray layer of dust had accumulated on the furniture. Apparently Waymon's attention to yard work did not extend to the interior. Waymon returned from the kitchen and shoved a beer at Ray, who settled into the chocolate sofa. He left the beer on the table: a bit early to start drinking.

"Did you like working in San Francisco?" Ray asked.

"I reckon I did," said Waymon, rubbing his palms together. "Been here long enough. I like Southern California more. I like the heat. I was thinking of moving to San Diego, but it's turning into another LA."

"Too noisy," offered Ray.

"Too noisy. And too many people. SeaWorld is taking over Mission Bay. They sell everything at SeaWorld now! When Shamu dies, they'll sell his pecker as a yard ornament."

"Anyway, I've been here since the 70s. It's home. San Francisco was different then. The drug culture swamped the city. Lots of wide-eyed innocents. Haight-Ashbury drew 'em west, people coming here because they saw hippies dancing beneath a fucking street sign on the six o'clock news!"

"People change their lives because of the things they see on TV," Ray said. Waymon looked unhappy at the interruption. He continued.

"By 1969, the dealers took over the neighborhoods. The emphasis in Haight-Ashbury was on the H-A-T-E. Not a pleasant place. Not really peace and love. When these wad stains saw a hippie, they jacked him up. They got these kids hooked on narcotics, and then took 'em for all they were worth."

Waymon spoke with a slight Southern accent, a relic of his youth in North Carolina. He showed a certain sunken charm, suspiciously friendly as only cops can be. A talented detective, he had been considered a great partner, albeit eccentric. He worked some of the toughest beats, and had more than his share of good press. But his offbeat demeanor was seen as a less desirable trait in a supervisor, and so he had been relegated to working his entire career as a vice detective. And Waymon knew it; knew he had been tagged with some invisible stamp of noncompliance. But he never cared about a promotion. He scorned his fellow officer's willingness to accept mediocrity in exchange for a pompous title when hair turned white and bellies grew soft.

"Waymon, I don't know what Dominique told you about this case. I'm looking for a girl who disappeared about ten years ago. Her family's lawyer asked me to try to track her down. She was last known to be living here in the 1990's. She may have been a prostitute."

"You happen to have a photo?"

Ray pulled out the photo of Tania. "Her name is Tania Kong. She would be twenty-eight now."

Waymon took the picture, and turned it in his thick hands. "Hmm. Pretty girl. Never seen her. I can run her name by someone at the station, see if she was ever arrested."

Ray watched Waymon, who seemed to be perpetually squinting. As if his eyes were rimmed with the grime of criminals spewing lies at him for a quarter century. He wondered how many suspects the man had interrogated and bashed down over the years.

"I know that she was arrested at least once," said Ray. "I checked court records. There was a 1997 arrest for prostitution in Chinatown."

"How long was she working?"

"I don't know. The fact she worked at all was news to me. And I don't think my client had any idea."

Waymon scratched his nose absentmindedly. "You suspect she's still working?"

"I don't know. Where do the girls work usually?"

"Well, most of 'em are on the internet." Waymon opened his fingers to show cyberspace. "They have web sites now. But the city has several areas where street girls can still be found. Some guys just like drive-by pussy."

"Where is the drive-by pussy in this city?"

"You've got your downtown girls, mostly on Geary and O'Farrell near Jones. They get to be thick as flies on a weekend night. Some of them are known to wander up to Post, but the folks there are more active — shoo 'em off right quick. Shemales work the corner of Larkin and Post. Is she a real girl?"

"I have no reason to suspect any unusual surgeries," Ray said.

"Good. They give me the creeps, those trannies — 'You wanna go with me baby?'" Waymon imitated a falsetto voice. "Disgusting."

"Anywhere else?"

"The Mission has a tittering of hookers on 16th. Roughest corner in the city. Young girl out there at 2 AM, she looks forty-five by morning. Classic crack whores. Drier than a nun's twat."

"You have a lovely way with words."

Waymon shrugged. "Regional aptitude, Ray. All southerners know how to work their way around a word. "

Waymon sipped his beer. All the windows in the house were closed. The room was cooking, but Waymon looked perfectly comfortable. Ray looked around at a number of photographs on the walls. Some appeared to be crime scene photos.

"And don't forget the house girls," Waymon added. "Like I said, they all have web sites now. Trolling for clients on the web. Real discreet. Hell, some of those sites are better than IBM."

Ray glanced around the room and settled briefly on a framed picture of Richard Nixon. Waymon noticed his gaze.

"Here, let me show you something." Waymon got up suddenly. He wiped dust from a bureau and retrieved something from a drawer. He returned with a signed photo showing Richard Nixon shaking hands with a newly minted police officer. The caption read: *President Nixon presents award to Detective Waymon A. Pierce, May 2, 1971.* Nixon's face, frozen in a smile deeper than sainthood.

"Nixon's about the greatest president this nation has ever had. He did wonderful things with the Chinese. He walked on the Great Wall. He looked them in the face and said: 'Be our friends or we'll bomb the whole billion of you back to the Stone Age. Knock down the Great Wall too.' He was a great man."

Ray listened as Waymon launched into a survey of Nixon's foreign policy objectives circa 1971.

Let him ramble, thought Ray. He moved the conversation back to where he wanted to go: "Waymon, do you know if there were any detailed records of the arrest? Did you normally fingerprint or photograph the girls?"

Waymon nodded. "Yes, we photographed every girl we arrested. More of a public service than anything. These girls were lost, runaways. End up on the bottom of the Bay if they're not careful. We wanted to help the families track 'em down." He paused. "Let me show you something."

Waymon picked up a jagged piece of gray rock from a table. "This is asbestos in its natural form. I found it once while panning for gold. It's completely harmless in nature. But heat it, process it, put it on the side of your house — one speck in your lungs, you're one plot down from the Marlboro Man."

Waymon got up. Ray followed him into a tan kitchen. An eerie mix of old and new haunted the place: a 1950s avocado refrigerator, a juicer on the counter next to a pile of orange pulp. A woman hadn't been in this place in decades.

They took the stairs down into the cellar. Lights blinked on automatically, revealing a minor disaster area of cardboard boxes, a canvas heavy bag, boxing gear, an old table, and numerous filing cabinets of different sizes and shapes: wood cabinets, old steel behemoths, newer ones in anodized black. There was a dime store Indian made of wood, various paintings in ornate gold frames, stacks of old porno magazines, and a Halloween decoration of a witch on a broom. Waymon waded into the piles, blowing dust, moving boxes. "I know it's here. I knooooow it's here," he said. After about five minutes, he dragged out two boxes, looking pleased.

"When I retired from the force, they were just tossing old cases, including misdemeanor mugs. Even some of the older felonies, back to the 60's, all ready to be tossed away. I took it all! It's not in any kind of order, just box loads of criminals and degenerates. You're welcome to sort through it."

Waymon pointed to a work bench running along one wall. "You can work there. Just don't take anything without checking with me first!" he said. Then he turned and headed back up stairs.

Ray pulled one box closer to him and carried it to the work bench. Various nude photos of women decorated the walls, some of them looking like they had been pinned for decades on the nails of Waymon's lust.

Ray opened the box and peered inside. There were rows of old photos, curled at the sides with graying edges. Snapshots of grifters, murders, arsonists, rapists. The faces of men in various snaky, blunt, angry poses. The overwhelming maleness of crime seeped from the pictures. It was all neatly cataloged: the local San Francisco purveyors of vice, labeled with notes and accompanied by a photograph.

He looked quickly through the box. The pictures from the 1960s were all black and white, the faces poignant in monochrome stillness. Some faces peered out with a look of sanctified surprise, as if asking: "Do my crimes still matter?" Others showed men with a self-conscious bent of the head as they held up a sign with inmate numbering, forced to assist in their own degradation. The hardcore felons just glared, bleak and shark-eyed. Arsonists wore the most disturbing look: a vacant gaze, faintly sexual.

The pictures were sorted roughly by year, filed by a court docket number. After rummaging for a few hours, Ray found mug shots of prostitutes from the 1960s.

Ray looked at the photos. One girl, a bruised face set with eyes that were elfin and sprightly. She wore a stiff collared dress that reminded him of dancers he had seen on old TV shows like Laugh-In. An older black woman, looking off to her left, the picture faded, blurry, like a jazzy snapshot of a Harlem after-hours club. A Midwestern farm girl with heavy-rimmed glasses that made her look like a high school math teacher.

He wondered what had become of the women. Dead probably. He knew of a famous Boston call girl known as the Leopard Lady on account of a spotted coat she usually wore while picking up johns in the theater district. Supposedly she married a high-tech mogul in the western suburbs. The exception. The mug shots, so different than the ones of the men, capturing a strange feminine disregard for the cop—it had probably been a man—taking the picture. Almost like they never saw him, looked through him. A sliver of terrible light in those eyes. Not innocence, but something else, a grim illumination. He felt a sadness looking at the photos, but there was something else too, something almost holy. He could not stop poring over the faces.

Waymon had quite a collection, Ray thought. He spent over an hour before finding a stack of color photos from the 1990's. They were smaller, laid out on a page according to case number. He peered through several pages of photos.

He recognized her immediately, the intelligent eyes gleaming even in a mug shot, the tender mouth. Ray flipped over the photo, and read: Tania Kong: DOB 04/26/73; 639 Jones Street, Apt. 12, San Francisco, CA. Charge CPC 309.

Ray sat back, very pleased. He peered through a few more photos, but found none of Tania. He looked around at the chaos—boxes, photos, the musty pleasures of an old basement. He walked upstairs to find Waymon sitting on one of his atrocious brown sofas.

"What did you find?"

Ray flapped a photo he held in his hand. "Mind if I make a copy of this?"

"Sure. You had some luck. Good. I never throw out anything, you know. I'm a pack rat of the first order."

Ray handed Waymon the photo. He studied it for a moment. "Nope, never met her. Even if I met a million like her." He handed the photo back to Ray. "You can have it."

Ray took the photo, thanked Waymon, and then left.

Chapter 10

R ay raced back to San Francisco over the Bay Bridge. The morning grayness had burned off, leaving the sky blue and wide. Treasure Island loomed as he entered the tunnel, then the gray jigsaw of downtown skyscrapers, and the pale upraised finger of Coit Tower to the north. In the distance, the Marin Headlands shouldered its rocky bluffs into the sun-ripped Pacific.

He exited on Bryant and headed up 8th Street to Taylor, took a left on Eddy, and drove toward the library.

The San Francisco Public Library, a fog-gray granite and glass monolith, was designed by an architect renowned for working with expansive rotundas and soaring spaces of light. Unfortunately, he was not a librarian. Once the library opened, his design was discovered to have left very little room for books. Nonetheless, the building emitted light like a shooting star, and even if people frequently searched in vain for a book, they all paused to admire themselves in the various reflective surfaces of the library.

He walked to the reference room. Rows of old phone directories, maps, heavy volumes of government documents that no one ever seemed to read. Ray pulled reverse directories for the early 1990's, and sat down at a table. He reviewed the resident listings for 639 Jones Street, Apartment 12. The 1996 directory listed a T. Kong in Apartment 12. It also listed Steven Moran as a tenant. He jotted down the name, and headed back toward the lobby.

He exited the library, blinking in the sun. Might as well try Moran on Jones Street now; it was a beautiful day. He walked up Larkin Street past sub shops, jewelry stores, and cheap bars. Located on the outskirts of the Tenderloin, Larkin bustled with commercial activity, most of it legal. An ethnic medley walked around him. Laden with groceries, old ladies hurried from the Vietnamese markets; a black man sold a motley collection of merchandise in front of an electric switching station; a young man with a grungy haircut wandered into a bookstore, looking for the meaning of life. Ray took a right on Bush Street and saw a drunk stagger out of a corner pool hall. Bracing his hands on a light pole, the drunk promptly heaved his afternoon libations onto a tree.

639 Jones was halfway down on the left side, a boxy, blue thirty-unit apartment building with Victorian adornments long since left to rot. The building was in a neighborhood on the lower section of Jones. It was the perfect spot for vice, where the steaming muck of the Tenderloin lapped the shores of Nob Hill decency.

The steel security door was ajar. Ray slipped inside and looked at the mailboxes. Apartment 12 was labeled "resident," with no name listed. A sure sign of criminal activity. The inner door was locked. Ray paused and picked up a newspaper, loitering in the hall. He thought he loitered well. He was considering the next spoke in the investigative wheel when the inner door opened and an Asian woman in jeans and a red leather jacket stepped out. She held the door. Thanking her, Ray entered.

The hallway was painted institutional white. Wall sconces with flame-shaped amber bulbs cast a lurid hue. Debris littered the hallway: bottles with cigarette butts sloshing in the swill, condom wrappers, coffee cups. A sign on the wall read:

Management will not help settle gambling debts. Gamble at your own risk. Thank you. Manager.

He geared up for the upcoming interview. Numerous scientific studies had been conducted in the field of psychology regarding the detection of deceptive behavior. For a time, experts taught that if a person's eyes shifted right, he was creating a visual response (and therefore presumably lying);

if the person looked left, he was recalling an actual event (and thus most likely telling the truth). Newer studies had concluded that these eye movement theories were utter crap. If a man blinked, he was nervous, or stressed, or he had a gnat caught under his left eyelid; if he sweated profusely, he was lying, or possibly had lived for several years in Finland.

The heavy wooden door of apartment 12 was straight ahead. Ray knocked. A minute passed. The door opened a crack and an Asian man peered out. He was in his 30's, black hair styled with angular aggression in a crewcut.

"Hi, is Steven here?"

The face gave no flicker of recognition. "Um, no."

"I'm looking for Steven Moran. I thought he lived here. Do you know him?"

No answer.

"I'm trying to reach him." Ray took a leap. "How about Tania, is she in today?"

The man continued the stony look, but Ray saw a subterranean ripple, just around the eyes. The man recognized the name.

"Can't help you. But please, wait a minute." The man said please awkwardly, as if not accustomed to polite words.

Noise of steps padding across a wood floor. Silence. Then a new face at the door, Asian, same haircut, a lank, wary face.

"What do you want." Said not as a question, insistent.

"Hi, I'm trying to reach Steven Moran."

"Who are you?" the man asked.

"Ray Infantino. I'm a friend."

"You mentioned someone else," the man said.

"Tania Kong." Ray jabbed the guy with a look.

"Do you have a card?" He was friendly, the new guy, smiling a big Sunday afternoon smile. Ray handed him a card. The man looked at the card. "A local number?"

"That number is the best way to reach me." He was not in the habit of providing hotel numbers. "Do they still live here?"

"No. They moved."

"Do you have an address?"

"No. Sometimes we get mail for them. But if we can get word to them." He trailed off. "If we see them."

"I'm sure you will. On both counts." Ray smiled.

The Asian man closed the door, grinning or grimacing, it was tough to tell. Ray turned and walked away,

Ray heard the door click open. He turned around. Inside the crack of the door, he could see dark clothing and a sliver of face. An eye appeared, oddly disjointed in the narrow aperture. The he heard whispering. The door closed again abruptly after a few seconds. The hallway was still.

Ray did not like the hallway all of a sudden, and he walked toward the stairway.

Outside, he looked at the building but he couldn't determine if the apartment had any windows facing the front or side alley. Probably not—the apartment seemed to be located to the rear.

Well, something was set in motion. He had no idea what.

Ray decided to walk a few blocks to his old apartment in North Beach. He walked up Nob Hill, past Grace Cathedral and Huntington Park. Children on swings, flying into the blue sky, while across the street, luminaries and tourists waded into the throngs in the lobby of the Fairmont Hotel. He headed north on Mason and dropped down a block over to Powell Street on the edge of Chinatown. Shabby restaurants with dusty corn plants in the window. He crossed over to Washington Square and walked on Powell Street, stopping in front of a vintage clothing shop. He looked over at the apartment building across the street where his old life had burned away.

The building had been rebuilt—no lot stood vacant for long in the city, where real estate was always in short supply. The facade was painted bright white, which highlighted the red tile roof. Ray wondered if any of his old neighbors still lived there—probably so. He wasn't sure if he wanted anyone to see him.

He often dreamt of his old home on Powell Street. The sun streamed on maple floors; he used to lie on the floor, basking in the heat and listening to music. He kept his eyes closed: then you heard the music like it was meant to be heard. But now the sun scorched his face. Memories were alive in a way they should never be. He walked through the burning rooms. Looking for her. A voice in the smoky misery. He had left the apartment, their apartment, walked to the corner store. Routines carved over years. She teased him about drinking the last cup of tea. "Pick up some tea, OK?" Her last words as he went out. There's an alleyway you'll walk into for the last time. You'll drink from a cup you'll never touch again.

Ray turned for a second, thought he recognized a woman crossing the street. A bus raced up Powell and blew diesel gusts into his face. He walked around the corner and headed to the North Beach playground. Kids were playing basketball. A group of young children jumped in the pool with their parents. He sat on a low wall, and watched kids in the playground kick soccer balls off a concrete wall. The echo of each shot boomed in his belly: pow pow pow pow pow.

JOHN F. NARDIZZI

Chapter 11

She knew they were watching for her. Not safe walking in the city. Too many Triad soldiers roaming the streets, ready to snuff out her daylight. She was exhausted. The city looked sick to her. Dismal pavement everywhere, no trees, a chill hardness in passing faces. But she needed to get outside. The acrid air of the apartment was killing her. She needed to think.

She took a cab out to the park, directing the driver along Fulton, away from the noodle shops in the Chinese neighborhoods near Clement. Dressed in a sweatshirt and faded jeans, she looked like just another disheveled lump moving in the anonymous morning gray.

She got out of the cab near the greenhouse in Golden Gate Park. Lots of tourists and joggers. A carefree babble in the air that she remembered from long ago. She pulled her baseball cap down low over her face.

The air was cool in the western section of the city, sheltered with trees and fog. To a city girl, the oxygen was almost intoxicating. She meandered along the grass, staying just behind a group of four older men talking about the 49ers. They strolled well off the main roads and she carefully followed, padding her way through the dewy lawn. The group passed by Spreckels Lake and approached the horse stables. She felt better, took a huge breath of cool ocean air.

A luxury car was parked near the entrance to the stables. Two Chinese men in dark clothes sat inside. Tania froze and almost stopped, her belly cold and heavy. She watched them from behind her sunglasses. Not sure if they were Triad soldiers, but stopping or turning abruptly would be too noticeable. She kept walking.

The group of 49er fans moved on and she stayed with them. The air shimmering now with anticipation. She could hear voices calling from the soccer fields beyond the trees. The men in the car were watching the road. But with her hair cut so short, the cap, they would never notice her.

She was shaking all over. The thing they did that night. Cindy shot in the back, Jesus sweet Jesus, the guy came up on her so sudden, just took her out.

Tania pulled abreast of the car. One of the men gestured. They looked down at something. Tania picked up her pace. She saw the passenger side door open. A short Chinese man stepped out. His eyes were hawking her now. He stepped around the door for a closer look

Her nerves fired in an adrenal surge. Then she sensed rather than saw him moving away from the car. His eyes layered into her across the car hood. Hands fluttering out in front of her, she jogged past the car to the group of men ahead of her, calling urgently to them—"They're following me, oh God, you gotta help me—"

The men saw her distress and stopped in the road. Heads turned back to face the two gangsters coming up the road.

Pop-pop pop echoed in the trees. One of the men fell instantly. Shots continued as the rest scattered. Tania raced up the hill. A voice was screaming and she knew then it was hers. The two Triad soldiers sprinted toward her. She glanced back and saw their pursuit was interrupted — one of the men from the group threw something, a bottle or can, something heavy enough to slow them for a second.

Tania bounded over a pine bluff and raced down toward a wide green lawn at the Polo Fields. There were dozens of people playing soccer on several fields. She raced across the nearest field, right through a game. Voices yelling at her, "What the fuck!!"

The men were following. A voice yelled: "He's got a gun."Everyone scattered. To Tania, it looked surreal, semi-controlled chaos because of the colors of the teams: one blue and white, the other purple, the heedless, kindred colors running together and separately, away from the fields.

Damp and slick grass below her feet. She was panting now, gasping for oxygen, her limbs electric with fright. She tore across another field and glanced back, her face stretched into a wide-eyed terror mask.

The men jogged behind her. They were heavy, thank god, and they were too far back — for now — to shoot her in the back. Cindy in the hotel, they just walked up and shattered her spine.

The smell of cut grass. People perched on the crest of the natural earthen wall that bordered the fields. Some were cowering while others held hands to heads. Calling 911 — she could hear sirens in the distance.

Blue lights twinkled far off amidst the eucalyptus trees. Tania's breath came in gasps. She raced after a small contingent of purple clad soccer players heading pell mell into the trees. Quieter under the trees. She ran and ran, the lactic acid building and building, slamming upward, past the limits of her muscles. She lurched the last few feet toward a knoll, then toppled over the edge into a hole near a tree.

Fog drifted into the cool dell. The scent of damp pines, leaves, dirt. The sun sneaked down below the tree line. The sirens faded off to her left, back near the field. No one was around. She slumped down and lay still.

Someone was watching. She opened her eyes. A black shape stood at the edge of the dell. One of the Triad soldiers. He peered through the trees, but he wasn't sure where to go. Locked his dark eyes on a clump of trees and undergrowth where she lay. He stepped toward Tania.

Then a siren came closer, some distance to the right. The solider paused, uncertain, looking off into the distance. He looked back down, then a cold smile slashed across his face. The siren blared closer. The man stepped back, turned right and disappeared.

Chapter 12

Ray walked back to his hotel. Windy and cool now. He and Dominique had agreed to meet for a late dinner. He called her at work.

"Well, good afternoon."

"Let me take you to dinner at the Grand Cafe at the Hotel Monaco."

"Two calls in one week, Ray."

"You were an agreeable dinner companion last night," he said.

"You were somewhat agreeable yourself."

She always had a wonderful sense of humor, he realized, a trait he had somehow forgotten.

"Did you see Waymon?"

"Yes, I did. Ornery old coot, but he panned out big-time."

"Tell me."

"He's a pack rat. Never tosses anything," Ray said. "He had mug shots of the girl I'm looking for."

"That's great. I knew he'd help you."

"I'll fill you in at dinner, if you can meet." Ray picked at some lint on his pants.

"What time is good for you?" she asked.

"7:00 PM. I'll meet you there."

"See you then." They said goodbye.

Ray hung up the phone. He flicked on his computer and logged into the locator databases. He needed to find Moran, the guy who had lived with Tania. And deal with whatever was happening at the apartment on Jones Street. Jettison into the vagueness, bang on people's doors. Decipher a person's eye-blink, the way they intoned the word "No".

He ran several searches for Steven Moran, finding five different individuals with that name within the city limits.

In Marin, he found three more. But only one of the guys had a past address on Jones Street in San Francisco—Steven H. Moran, age twenty seven, currently at 49 Vallejo Street, Apartment 1. He felt certain that this was the right guy. It was late. He would pay a visit to Mr. Moran tomorrow.

After clipping the .32 semiautomatic on his belt, Ray walked down to the lobby and out to Jones and Sutter. He headed west and stopped at Last Man Standing Saloon, a local place where he had spent many nights. He loved the stripped-down blues bands that played here. A poster advertised a band he had seen many times, The Acolytes, playing for the next three nights. A guitarist, a bassist, and a heroin addict drummer who drifted into the world of the living just long enough to bestow his percussive blessings on a drumbeat crowd. He would have to take Dominique here.

The evening had grown bracingly cool. The last rush hour traffic burst through the intersection, horns blaring. He walked a few blocks to the Hotel Monaco, and saw Dominique standing in the entrance. She wore a muted leopard skin outfit that fit her well.

"I envy the leopard," he said.

She smiled. "You like it? A bit wild, I know."

"Very few women can carry that off." He nodded approvingly.

He told her about his earlier visit to Tania's old Jones Street apartment.

"Be careful Ray. Don't you have someone with you when you go to these places?"

"Sometimes. But this place was fine."

Inside the restaurant, the host guided them to a table. They ordered a bottle of wine, a fine Malice.

"So how does it feel to be back?" Dominique asked.

"Strange. It's not my city anymore. I had a weird feeling today while I walked, thinking I might recognize someone. Like I always used to when I walked in the city. But I never saw anyone. And then it hit me that it's been ten years since

I lived here."

The waiter returned to the table with the wine. He was efficient and unobtrusive. After reading the menu description of shrimp swimming in a spicy tomato sea, Ray ordered scampi fra diavolo. Dominique ordered butterfish. They split a salad.

"Interesting salad," said Dominique. "What would life be without Sonoma greens?"

"That's what a salad evolves into when it costs $15.95," Ray said.

The food matched the exotic atmosphere of the restaurant. The Grand Cafe was resplendent, with pale yellow walls, soaring pillars and chandeliers with amber-hued glass. The pillars did not obscure Ray's view of two Asian men sitting at the bar. They rolled in shortly after he and Dominique. Both men were in their 20s, with dark jackets, hair cut short. One gazed over once too often to make it a coincidence.

He said nothing to Dominique — why spoil the butterfish? The waiter came by to refill the minute amount of water Ray had consumed.

Ray told her about Waymon and his odd collection. They ordered a nightcap of tea and Sambucca before calling for the check. The two Asian men continued to drink at the bar.

Ray walked behind Dominique and headed for the door. As they walked by the bar, the two Asian men continued to banter. Neither guy looked familiar. Ray slammed one man a hard look. The guy gave no response. Ray and Dominique continued walking. He held the door open, gazing back inside the restaurant. If the men had been tailing him, they were making no attempt to follow now.

Outside, the theater crowd, overdressed and hungry, was milling about and battling for cabs. Ray and Dominique stepped in a taxi that pulled curbside. Dominique directed the driver to Pacific Heights. Ray watched the rearview mirror to see if they were tailed, but no lights followed.

"Thanks for dinner."

Ray paused. "How are you for tomorrow?"

"Call me. Maybe we'll do something late," she replied.

"Good."

The cabbie met his gaze in the rearview, eyebrows raised slightly.

The cab drove down Jackson Street, and pulled next to a large white Mediterranean home. The rear of the house commanded a view of San Francisco Bay. Dominique stepped out. "I'll wait to hear from you tomorrow. Don't work too hard." She stepped out and walked toward her front door.

"Wait until she gets inside please," Ray said to the driver. He watched her walk into the foyer. After she stepped inside, Ray had the driver head back downtown. Bush Street was a row of green lights, and Ray was downtown within five minutes.

He was pleased with how things were going. Would have been nice to have been asked up to her place. But that way was madness. Slow was best.

"I'll get off at the corner of Jones." The taxi sagged to a stop, Ray got out, and paid the driver.

The night air was chilled with fog. He checked his watch: 11:10 PM. He walked down Jones, headed right on Sutter to the hotel. He passed a narrow alley and looked up, following the cramped passage up the hill, where it ended on the edge of California Street. Behind loomed the bluish black sky.

At the very edge of sight, where the street cut away from the dark sky, Ray saw a figure standing. Medium height, legs apart. Arms bunched in front. He saw a sudden flash of light, and then another. His gut coiled instinctively. But he quickly realized it wasn't gunfire. It was the flash of a camera. The figure stood facing downhill and took a series of photos.

The figure bent down, and Ray heard a tinkling sound as of coins dropping on concrete. As if beckoned offstage, the figure turned, walked quickly to the left, and disappeared behind the building.

Not moving, Ray stood and watched the hill. He thought

about following, but he was 50 yards away and the hill rose at a steep angle. He would be hard-pressed to chase down someone one block ahead and uphill. Plus the streets at the crest of Nob Hill broke off in numerous directions. And what had the person done other than take a picture? He did not dwell on the fact that someone was taking photos just before midnight.

He crossed Sutter and walked back to the hotel, moving deliberately, not hurrying. He looked up each street as he passed but saw no one. As he turned the corner at Jones Street, four hooded shapes jumped him. He crashed to the pavement. Pain erupted from his head—his ear was being ripped off. Heavy weight on his chest, someone held his arms. He felt a blizzard of kicks and punches pounding everywhere. A boot veered toward his face and he offered his shoulder instead. A bolt of pain shivered his arm. "Fuck him up!" a voice muttered.

He stopped struggling for a second. Then with all the power he could summon, he spun quickly on the ground. He leg was free and he whipped his foot into a meaty leg; a cry of pain rang out. The simple maneuver caught them by surprise, and he saw momentary light, men above him. A weakness in group attacks — someone let up, thinking the fight was over. He kicked out again wildly, and the kick glanced off someone's shin. A momentary break, two of the men now moving uncertainly.

An engine roared, and he knew they were going to run him down. Then a voice: "Don't hit him, just—" but then another voice broke in, clipped and guttural. Ray missed the words but the commanding tone was clear. The sound of boots thudding on the concrete. He felt water running in his eyes, but knew it was something else. A door closed and an engine died away in the distance.

Ray sat up. The whole thing had been ten seconds, maybe twenty. He hunched against the building and wondered about the last voice.

An old Chinese woman walked by and shot him a curious look. She kept plodding uphill. He must have looked like a bum, rolling in his filth. A five second transformation. He laughed in spite of himself, a half-mad cackle.

Two women, middle-aged, neatly dressed in identical jackets, were coming at him now.

"Oh my god, are you OK? What happened sir?"

He stood still as his head tried to find equilibrium. Blood ran from a cut above his left ear.

"Not sure. Welcome to California."

"You need us to call an ambulance?"

He struggled up. "I'd settle for dinner right now."

One woman smiled.

"You're OK. You're joking."

"Sure. No ambulance needed."

"You sure? You sure look like you can use some help."

"People die in ambulances. I'll be fine." He stood up, stretched his back. "Did you get a look at the guys who did this to me?"

"Big guys. Chinese. God, I hope you don't need me to ID them. They all look the same to me."

Ray sighed, looking at the two ladies in their matching coats.

"Get a license plate number?"

"No, sorry." One of the ladies gave him a corner of a smile. "I don't see so good anymore. Do you need help getting home?"

"I can get back now, I'm staying one block away." His jacket was ripped and blood leaked out of the hole on his right pant leg. Ray limped back down the hill to Sutter. It could have been a lot worse. He had been completely surprised, badly outnumbered—he had a sense of four or five men dancing on his bones back there. Asians. He did not recognize what language they had spoken. He had his wits about him, no concussion, and relatively pain free—except for his shoulder. That would change with morning. His face had some abrasions, a cut above his ear, but nothing major. He knew Dominique would dote on him, so no need to cover those up too much.

Back in his hotel room, he took a long hot bath. When he was done, he took a seat near the window. He kept the lights off. He stared down into the street, which was still alive with neon signs and nighttime traffic. Steam drifted from a manhole cover, the exhalation of a dying city night. He wondered why steam still drifted from manholes in the 21st century. A scene he had witnessed in countless old movies. Sewer technology should have improved, but there it was. He liked the steam.

No one looked up from the street to his window. After a half hour, he crawled into bed, sleep rolling down slowly from above.

JOHN F. NARDIZZI

Chapter 13

The next morning, Ray awoke to another sunny day in California, the kind that keeps the myth alive. His entire body throbbed with pain. He gulped down some ibuprofen. He put on a blue dress shirt with a dark blue patterned jacket, set off with a gold tie and tan pants. Then he dialed room service. An overly polite waiter set a table with scrambled eggs and a pot of black coffee.

Ray ate quickly and then got ready to see his witness. He put a notebook in his leather bag, along with two pens — the weaponry of conversation. He planned to stop in North Beach and interview Steven Moran this afternoon. Most witnesses talked when approached for an interview. They were concerned or curious or bored. Some wanted to test wits; others needed a break from their padded lives. Even when their self-interest cried out for the quietness of the grave, they talked. And if the questioner donned a jacket and tie, worthiness was beyond question.

He exited the hotel, walked up the hill, and caught a cab on California Street. The city was in the throes of morning rush hour. He directed the driver to Vallejo Street in North Beach.

North Beach was the old Italian neighborhood of San Francisco. Over the years, North Beach had turned into an annex of Chinatown: Chinese residents were now a solid majority. But the Italian flavor remained in the commercial area, diluted but lingering, the scent of garlic and tomato sauce wafting from the restaurants lining Columbus Street. Dressed in coats and ties, old Italian men tossed crumbs to pigeons in Washington Square and drew on an endless reservoir of gestures, hands swooping like brown doves. They patrolled the perimeter of the park; they held ancient grudges; they sat for three hour lunches and played bocce near the library. They were the last of a generation that had not renewed itself.

Ray got off at the corner of Vallejo and Grant and walked to 49 Vallejo Street. The house was midway up Telegraph Hill, a six unit Georgian-style building with a view of the concrete canyons of downtown. The small yard was dominated by an enormous century plant, its green spiky leaves scarred with the carved initials of passersby. 'Moran' was listed on the mailbox, apartment 2. He rang the bell. No one answered. He rang again. Nothing. He waited for a minute and then walked back to North Beach.

Ray headed over to Cafe Trevi, owned by his old friend, Nino Pescatore. The 68 year old still served his signature dish of spinach ravioli at the Cafe on the corner of Stockton and Columbus. He was a legend in the area, holder of special titles, privy to neighborhood secrets. He embodied the old neighborhood as North Beach underwent a creeping metamorphosis from Italian to Chinese.

As head of the Italian American Sports Club, Nino was the honorary chairman of the Columbus Day Parade, a position that included the right to play Christopher Columbus during the celebration. Things had gone roughly as of late. A few years ago, he had expected to land a replica of the Santa Maria at Fisherman's Wharf in a reenactment of Columbus's landing in the New World. Unfortunately, his landing was met by protesters decrying the destruction of Native American culture. Despite Nino battering several protesters with a foil-wrapped replica of Columbus's sword, he was ultimately prevented from landing. He had vowed to land—whatever the cost—this year.

Nino sipped a cappuccino with Ray at a small table near the window. "This year, there will be no problems. I have everything accounted for."

"What are you going to do?"

"We are going right for the top. Cut off the head." Nino smiled.

"Sounds drastic."

"Go for the jugular. Choke 'em out early. I told the nuts if they don't screw around with the landing, we'll send something over. Give 'em a big envelope."

"An envelope?"

"A donation. For their cause. Why not?" Nino shrugged. "Listen, I'm Sicilian, I feel for these guys. The Lucchese in North Beach, they were here first. Goddamn Italian blue-bloods. They called us Sicilians the mud people when we came here. I know how people get. Just don't protest when I land. That's the message that was delivered." Nino paused. "They protest that hard when the real Columbus came, maybe we never have this conversation."

"Did you really smack someone with that sword?"

Nino gave him a look of mock horror. "The guy slipped. Salt water, people spill things." He sipped his cappuccino daintily, three fingers jutting like antennae.

"Why do you sip like that?" Ray asked.

"Like what?"

Ray mimicked Nino's splayed fingers.

"What? You want to talk about fingers? That's how it's done. Balance the cup. Ergonomics."

Ray nodded. "Nino, I'm trying to reach a guy who lives up the street. Steven Moran. Do you know him?"

"Yeah, I know Steven. Came in this morning."

"Any idea where he works?" asked Ray.

"He's working at home, I think. He's a researcher or something. He should be there now."

"OK, I'm heading up there again. I already tried him, but no one was there."

"He's there. Funny guy, probably saw your mug and decided he's not answering," said Nino. "Try him again."

The two men watched street action, the usual city plumage. A blond entered wearing a black dress and open-toed heels.

"I don't like long middle toes on a woman," said Nino, smoothing the air with his fingers. This was obviously a topic close to his heart. "But she looks good. She has the toes to carry off the look."

"All-star toes," said Ray. "If the middle toe slithers off the shoe, that's it for me."

"Yes. I know exactly what you mean," said Nino. "I'm seeing a lot of second-tier toes."

"Too many women are not paying attention to this," said Ray.

"Tell me about it," said Nino. "And young guys wearing these cheap sandals. Brutal, these guys. I'm serving the best expresso in the city to who? Some kid with plastic feet. The things I see."

The men said their goodbyes. Nino unshifted the charm and went to serve the blond.

Ray left the cafe and headed back up to 49 Vallejo. He rang and rang, leaning on the bell. This time the intercom came alive.

"Hello?"

"Steven Moran, please." Said Ray.

"This is him."

"Steven, my name is Ray Infantino. I'd like to speak with you regarding Tania, Tania Kong."

A long pause. "Who are you?"

"I'm trying to reach her on behalf of a family member."

"Who?"

"It'll just take a few minutes."

A few seconds passed. Then a buzzer sounded and the front door unlocked. Ray entered a brightly lit hallway devoid of any decoration. He heard a door open somewhere down the hallway and saw a head jut from the right into the hallway.

Ray walked toward the head. The head moved. Then a thin man with unkempt brown hair entered the hall. His jaw line had little definition, sloping into his neck, giving it a hoggish aspect, pink and soft. He wore a white tee-shirt and faded blue jeans.

Steven Moran shook Ray's hand, and invited him inside. Steven was in his forties, and wore his hair long in back. His bearing tilted toward the deferential—a guy who apologized after farting in an empty room. Originally from the East Coast, he gave off an aura of stumbling amazement, as if his soul had yet to adjust to the open spaces of the west.

"How did you find me?" Steven asked.

"I knew Tania once lived on Jones Street. You were listed there as a co-tenant."

"No, I mean here?"

"On Vallejo? Databases. If you spend money, then you are probably in the data."

Steven gestured to a seat, and Ray sat in a large green chair with a matching ottoman. "I hope I'm not bothering you," Ray said, knowing full well he was, and not caring at all.

Steven grinned. "Tania, what a blast from the past. I haven't seen her in years."

JOHN F. NARDIZZI

Chapter 14

The room smelled stuffy. Ray glimpsed a dingy pile of flannel shirts on the floor. Prints hung on the walls, pop art drawings of women or tropical beaches, stuff usually seen in health clubs and dentist's offices. The featured reading material was TV Guide, set neatly in the middle of the table. A halogen floor lamp tilted dangerously on the carpet, promising facial injuries to anyone sitting on the white sofa. The room's notable lack of personal effects made it strangely memorable, some horrific bodysnatching nightmare. Who really lived here?

Steven excused himself, took a piss, and returned to his spot on the sofa. His body looked soft as oatmeal; he hadn't pushed it since high school.

"Why are you looking for Tania again?"

"Her family is concerned about her. They haven't heard from her in years." Ray paused. "How did you get to know Tania?"

"Met her in a club. Best girlfriend I ever had." Steven sat back and sighed. He looked ready to unburden himself of some baggage. Ray decided to just sit back and let the man unwind.

In 1990, Steven had moved to San Francisco from Brooklyn. He embraced the open atmosphere that pervaded the city. He met superstars of remote art forms: Jade Vortex, a fire-breathing stripper; Pamela, whose one-woman show in South of Market warehouses involved her feeding live armadillos with organic pineapple held in her labia. He had fallen into the underground club circuit, where various groups rented out warehouses on weekend nights and threw raves that lasted into the early morning hours. Steven reminisced as he sat splayed on his sofa. "For two months I just smoked dope and partied. And I was actually meeting girls, good-looking ones too. I dated 40 year old women who educated me in ways I had not considered."

One night he attended a party on Townsend Street with a friend. As he sipped a beer, he saw an Asian woman walk to the bar. She was tanned, about five feet tall. Her black hair was streaked with blond. Her face had a regal sadness to it, a touch of wisdom that lifted just another face into stardom. Her name was Tania.

"She really put the hooks in me. I mean, look, I know I'm not the best looking guy—why kid myself? And I usually don't bother with the best looking girls—boring women who look good but have nothing to say. But there was something so seductive about her. So I talked to her. Even a blind hen gets a seed now and then."

"And how did the blind hen do this night?" Ray asked.

"Very well. I brought her a drink and made stupid jokes. She laughed at everything I said. We spent the night talking and dancing. She had lived in Hong Kong. She told me stories of her home. We left the club together at 3:00 AM. Everything went perfect, just one of those perfect nights."

After leaving the club, they saw a bus parked with its "Not In Service" sign lit; the driver was heading home for the night. Steven joked with the bus driver who, in a jovial midnight mood, took them on a wild careening trip over the steaming manhole covers of Kearny, up to the light show of Broadway. They got off the bus and ate seafood at You Lan. Afterwards, they went back to his apartment and screwed happily until dawn.

The next morning Tania was quiet, and she left quickly, refusing to have coffee or even accept a ride home. Steven had been reduced to begging for her telephone number, which she reluctantly gave. Steven leaned forward.

"After a few weeks of tea and coffee cake at four, I was frustrated. We couldn't go back to the mood of that first night. So she finally told me why she was acting so weird." He looked at Ray with a sharp nod, ready to divulge pivotal details. Showing his readiness, Ray opened his hands.

"She was an escort, a hooker. And she said that guys don't stick around for hookers."

"She told you that?" asked Ray.

"Yeah. That was why she was so cold—she thought that we could never have a relationship because of what she did."

"But you felt differently."

"Yeah, I was in love with her. She was a fabulous girl. She had a real sensuality." He sighed. "She must have been a great little whore."

Ray stifled a laugh. "When did you last see her?" he asked.

"I'm sorry, I was about to get to that. At that time, she had been living at the Hotel Virginia."

"Big brick place in an alley off Mason?"

"Right. She saw clients there, mostly businessmen."

"How did she get started in that business?" Ray asked.

"Tania told me she was working off debts owed by her parents. First she started working at the Peking Garden massage parlor. Eight girls, mostly Koreans. She was brought into the business by a girl who told her she was making 100 grand per year. All these girls lie about the amount of money they make, but that comes with the business." Steven sat back heavily.

"Did Tania live at the parlor? Ray asked.

"No."

"The Jones Street apartment?"

"That was her place. She moved there later." Steven's head swiveled energetically on its puffy neck stem. "After a time, I started spending more time at that apartment. He raised a finger. "You know you're serious when you have your own toothbrush in the crusty little holder at your girlfriend's house."

Ray nodded. "Sure sign. What did she tell you about her work?"

"That was a touchy subject for her."

"What do you mean?"

"She told me I didn't understand the business — she used a phrase 'in dark shadows.' Some Chinese colloquialism. And she was making a lot of money. She always had the hottest little outfits on — BeBe, Claiborne, you know the look. One of those Asian girls in little designer skirts strutting around the mall."

"I gave up hunting at the mall about twenty years ago," said Ray.

Steven grinned. "Not me. Anyway, a few months into it, the whole thing unraveled. I was tired of Tania screwing these guys. I told her to leave the life. I'd take care of her. But she refused. We had been drinking, and next thing you know, I'm shouting at her."

He left her apartment for the night, slamming the door hard on his way out.

The next afternoon Steven had returned to the apartment. He found three Asian men waiting.

"They lounged around. Like they owned the place. Tania sat on the floor in shorts and bare feet. She wouldn't even look at me."

When he tried to speak to Tania, one of the men pushed him back firmly. The other two men fired slight smiles his way. He smelt a faint whiff of violence on the horizon. A few more quick smiles and hands in bulging pockets underscored the sincerity of the new hosts.

"One of the men pulled all my clothes off my rack in the closet and shoved them in my hands. I was guided out." Steven slumped in his seat. "My last image of Tania was her sitting on the floor, completely devoid of any expression. She looked like a slave."

"Any idea of their connection to Tania?" Ray asked, trying to rope the increasingly melancholy man back into the sunlight of casual conversation.

"I think they were gangbangers. A protection racket. I remember reading about the Viet gangs and how they extort money from the legitimate businesses in the 'Loin."

"Did she call them?"

"I don't know. I don't think she did."

"Why do you think they were Vietnamese, and not Chinese?" asked Ray. "Did they identify themselves as Vietnamese?"

"No. I guess they could be Chinese."

"Do you know either language?"

"No." Steven paused. "That was the last time I saw her." He paged Tania that night and then numerous times the following day. She never responded. On a rainy Friday night, he donned a trench coat and took a cab over to Geary. The theater crowd, talking loudly, bellies stuffed with prix fixe dinners, filled the streets along with the working girls. Steven huddled beneath a tree on Jones, watching Tania's apartment for a sign of activity.

His efforts to find Tania died as desire flickered and grew dim. A beautiful piece of his life drifted into the shadows.

"To this day I regret not finding her. Maybe I regret meeting her." Steven's voice was low and disconsolate now. He picked at his shirt sleeve.

Ray asked again: "You never heard from her? Or saw her in the street?"

"Nothing."

"Did Tania ever mention any other names of people she hung out with?" Ray asked. "Friends or family?"

"No one except her friend, Moon," said Steven.

"She never mentioned her family?"

"No."

"Who is Moon?" Ray asked.

"I met her once at SF MOMA. I took Tania to a short photo exhibit there. Roy DeCarava, great black and white still shots from Harlem."

"I saw the DeCarava show. I liked the soulful scenes of empty kitchens."

"You saw it too? Great show." Steven paused. "Anyway, we stopped to talk to a friend of hers outside at the park."

Steven's face was looking more morose by the minute. He sank deeper into the cushions.

"Any last name?"

"Yi. Or Lee. I'm not sure."

"How old was she?"

"Late 20's. Long black hair, very hot. Superior genetics. She seemed tight with Tania, although I just met her that one time. They seemed to know each other well."

"Was she a working girl too?"

"Yeah. They don't use that term. Tania always referred to herself as a provider," Steven said, chuckling a bit.

"Where can I find this Moon Yi?" asked Ray.

"Or Lee."

"What?"

"Lee. Or it might be Li, with an 'i'."

"OK. How did they know each other?"

"I don't know. But they were close."

"Why do you say that?"

Steven dabbed a coffee stain on his shirt. "I don't know, something in the way they talked. Like a lot of preliminary stuff had already been discussed. Immediacy."

"Did Tania sleep with women?"

Looking more awake, Steven replied: "Not on a regular basis. If a client asked for it, she might double-team a guy. But in her personal life, I never saw any sign of it. That is a huge fetish for me, so believe me, I would have known. Seeing two girls together is a cleansing experience."

"I know what you mean," said Ray. "Any idea of where I can find Moon?"

"I remember Tania telling me Moon worked at the a spa in the Haight."

"Remember the name?"

"Mmmm, no." Steven thought for a moment. "Fuji Spa, maybe? I think that's it."

Steven sagged back in his chair, his back almost parallel to the floor.

"Steven, thanks for meeting. If you don't mind, I might call you again at some point to follow up on some things."

"You think you'll find her?"

"Hope so."

"You must have an interesting job."

"Usually. I get to see a wide selection from the menagerie. What do you do for a living?"

"I'm a programmer. I develop video games."

"Love video games. I spent a fortune playing Defender when I was young."

"Great game for its time."

Ray started toward the door.

Steve paused. "Can you let me know if you find her?"

Ray stopped walking and turned slightly. "Well, probably not. You can call me if you want; I'll let you know if she's all right. But I can't tell you where she is. Sorry."

"No, I understand." Ray said goodbye and jotted down Steven's phone number. Then Steven shut the door behind him.

Chapter 15

R ay headed for the stairs and considered his haul for the day. His peculiar personality aside, Steven Moran had been helpful: he had identified someone close to Tania, this woman named Moon.

Ray headed to Vallejo Street and walked down the hill to North Beach. He grabbed a seat outside Cafe Trevi and dialed Lucas Michael's office phone. He didn't like clients to get sticker shock. Progress meant time, and his time was on their dime. Michael's receptionist rang him through.

"I found a case for Tania in San Francisco. She was arrested on pandering and prostitution charges."

"Are we certain of this?" asked Lucas.

"Yes."

"That will be a bit of a shock," Lucas sighed. "Have you been able to locate her?"

"Not yet. I checked an old address that came up on a mug shot. She's no longer there — at least that was the story from the people at the apartment now. But I spoke with an old boyfriend of hers who had some interesting information." He relayed the main points of the Steven Moran interview, and let Lucas digest that unpleasant sampling. "Moran is quirky, but not a bad guy. He gave me what he could. I plan on meeting with a woman tomorrow who may have known Tania. I'll keep you posted."

"Who's the woman?"

"Moon. No last name yet — possibly Li. I'm working on it."

"Thanks Ray, good work. Look forward to hearing more."

They ended the call. Ray sat at the cafe, watching the mingled millions on the street. He decided that he would go see Moon immediately. Before he did, he wanted to get a start on the Project. He called Dominique.

"Nice to hear your voice," she said.

"Maybe some time soon, you can hear it live."

"We'll see, big boy." She laughed softly. "You might have to take me out one more time. I've seen all the tricks in your magic show. So what do you need now?"

"A number. Who did you recommend for surveillance here?"

I use the Perry Agency. I called him for you—Richard Perry, former Secret Service. He's very good, a lot more responsive than most of the retired cops out there." She checked her phone and gave him the number.

"I'll call you later today," he said.

Ray called the agency and got Richard Perry on the line. He outlined the history of Bobby Cherry. "The guy may be tied to other white supremacist groups operating on the West Coast—White Aryan Resistance, League of the South. I need to get him under surveillance for a few weeks. He lives in Oakland."

"Oakland!" said Richard. "That's odd."

"I know. He's stuck in a poor neighborhood with the very people he wants to shit on. How soon can you get on him?"

"Tonight if you want. Is he known to set up anywhere? Any destination?"

"He leaflets at the Wharf in San Francisco, Pier 39. You can find him there or at his home. I'll email you the details." Ray jotted down Richard's email address, and hung up the phone.

Ray thought Richard seemed OK. A bit amped up though; he would have to keep an eye on him. He composed a brief memo, and emailed it to him.

Chapter 16

Tania snipped and dark swaths of hair fell to the floor. She stared at her face in the cracked mirror. Her hair looked ratty; she hadn't styled it in weeks. Just another vagabond in another come-crusted motel somewhere north of the city.

She hacked at her hair again with the scissors. To anyone looking, she might be just a pretty ass Asian boi, a club kid in bad clothes. The problem was that there were dozens, maybe hundreds, of people looking for her. And some were looking hard. Every nerve in her body bristled with tension.

She finished cutting and looked at the mirror again. Looked like a dyke. That struck her funny, because although she had lustily buried her face between Moon's legs, she was not one of them. It was just that, when it came to beautiful men and women, she could not say no to love.

Tania took a sip of water from a plain glass. Felt a little better to be on the move in Marin County. San Francisco was too dangerous. She realized that she knew no one in the city. The men in her life were just paying customers, nothing more. Yes, some of them were kind and treated her well, very well in fact. And some fucked her good. A few had ventured close to becoming real friends. But she didn't always know their real names, and who was going to take a call now from a runaway whore under a death sentence? No one wanted that call. No one was riding into a fairy tale.

She went out, hooded as usual, staying away from any Asian restaurants or businesses. She walked across 4th Street to a little pizza joint and ordered a pizza, salad with ranch dressing and a Pepsi. An oily smell heavy in the air. All the Greek pizza places made dough that smelled the same. Some guy with dreadlocks sat in a booth and looking like he wanted to start a conversation. No way. She put on her iPod and wandered toward the door, staring out at the newspaper racks. Townie life rolled by quietly. She reached into her pocket and pulled out three quarters, bought the last copy of the local paper. Then her meal was ready. She zipped inside, picked up the paper bag and walked back for another lonely dinner inside her room.

She needed to set up something more permanent. These rooms were costing her a fortune. As she scanned the paper, she noticed an ad for a zen center. Free room and board in exchange for a commitment of time and work. The photograph in the ad showed the staff members beaming out goodwill and peace. That was something she could do. She laughed out loud. She was going from a working girl to a zen master in two weeks. Life was rich, she thought, devouring her salad. She hadn't eaten a full meal in days.

Chapter 17

Sitting at a Haight Street tacqueria, Ray ate a carnitas burrito and watched a fly-eyed street punk enter the store. Slime plastered the guy's warm-up jacket, and his eyes blinked rapidly. The guy moved to the salsa bar, looked around, then reached out and filled a few tiny paper cups with fresh salsa. He walked outside and handed the cups to a group of grubby kids sitting on the sidewalk. They were flying on glue and meth, and they devoured the salsa like it was sweet nectar. One of the restaurant owners, a young thick-shouldered Mexican, approached the group, who swore and moved away. "This is my business!" the restaurant owner yelled. "I got kids, man!" He walked by Ray, and shook his head.

"Hope it was the habinero," Ray said.

The owner laughed. "Ha ha, yeah! Burn their damn lips off. They wreck this place, man, taking all my stuff, the napkins, everything."

Haight-Ashbury. The scene of San Francisco's Summer of Love, acid-drenched streets and free-loving hippies cultivating enlightened philosophies and medieval hygiene. During the decades following the 1960s, the Haight had gotten edgier. Love may have flowed at one time, but now the street was often a sad parody of itself. Greasy-haired burnouts begged on street corners while young runaways chased feverish dreams among the ghosts of a summer now forty years dead. Occasional tourists wandered the street looking for free music and scantily clad California blondes. But some street corners showed resilience to the grime as young immigrants from Asia and South America opened new restaurants and shops. And Haight-Ashbury Music Center still bristled with Stratocasters and amplifiers for the fadeaway dreams of musicians.

Ray finished his dinner and headed up the street. He passed 63 Cole Street, the former residence of convicted murderer Charles Manson. Although the landlord tried to downplay the Manson angle, some tenants sought out the address, even paying a premium to live there and partake of some karmic convergence with the mass murderer.

He stopped at an orchid-colored Victorian, a two story Mansard with wood dentils and cornices accented with a number of different shades of purple and magenta. The paint was old and beginning to fleck and peel. A six-foot tall iron fence surrounded the property. A gate shaped in the likeness of a giant spider provided the only entryway. A green burst of exotic plants shadowed the windows, which were covered with heavy red drapery. A small metal sign over the basement door read "Fuji-Open". He rang the bell and waited.

Moon was probably not using her real name. She had been described by Moran as exceedingly gorgeous—he ought to notice that.

A small aperture in the door cracked open, startling him. A tiny face appeared: "Hi, you want massage? You been here before?"

"Yes."

The Lilliputian door closed.

The buzzer sounded, the door swung open, and he entered a gray hallway. An Asian woman of indeterminate age stood there, evaluating him with a stiff smile. She wore a tight black cocktail dress that accented her slim form; she had bare feet, and short hair over a face that, having seen forty years, still bore in the eyes a sliver of childlike grace.

"Who's working today?"

"Who you see before?

He slurred something that sounded like 'Lynn.'

"Who? Jen?" she asked, frowning.

"Yes. But I'd like to see everyone today."

She paused, smiling. "You want to see everyone? Ah, handsome man likes to shop."

Ray nodded and the girl disappeared. He heard some rustlings behind a screen, and the sound of skin being slapped into shape. He looked around. Neon lights, and a television blaring a Chinese language soap opera. He noticed a small sign on the wall that spelled out the rates, with a warning:

Prostitution is illegal in CA. Please do not ask for sexual services.

After a minute the girl returned, still smiling. "Here," she said, gesturing behind her.

Just beyond her hand stood three Asian women, all dressed in silk cocktail dresses showing legs and cleavage.

His eyes moved immediately to the woman on the end. She was heavily tanned, possibly Thai, with long black hair and perfectly formed features. She had a body that cried out for attention. She looked about thirty or so. The other two women were attractive as well, but he instinctively knew that the tan woman at the end was Moon.

Ray smiled ruefully, feeling suddenly on the spot: apparently he was now expected to dismiss two of the women. All had a readiness, a certain animal watchfulness to their eyes. These were not passive girls, although he did not doubt that they could convince a customer otherwise.

"I'd like all three" — the girls laughed politely — "but her first." He pointed to the lithe beauty on the end.

The two girls melted away. They would wait for other customers, the usual herd of pent-up men. They walked behind a screen and resumed listlessly watching the soap opera.

The girl locked eyes with him momentarily, smiled, and took his hand. She said nothing as she led him down a darkened hallway and into a room lit with a small table lamp. A massage table, a fan, several bottles of ointments, oils, powders and other liquid applications. White towels on a hook. The walls were covered with a print showing a spray of red flowers and several photographs.

Ray admired the girl's athletic body, barely concealed by her dress. She looked at him coolly: "You can take a shower and I'll be back. Would you like something to drink?"

Ray noticed that she spoke flawless English. "Water is fine. I didn't get your name."

"Vicky," she said. She left in a sparrow flight of silk.

Ray undressed. He adjusted the shower water, and stepped in, letting the hot water flood the fatigue out of his muscles. He finished, stepped out, wrapped a towel around him, and lay on the table. He smelled jasmine mixed with disinfectant. He looked closely around the room, which was decorated with what appeared to be the woman's personal effects: pictures of various people, a bamboo-framed painting showing a scene in a Oriental garden, and several long tapered candles.

Five minutes passed, and the woman returned, closing the door behind her.

She placed his water glass on a table next to him, and smiled. This was a well-rehearsed act for her, Ray thought, just another slab of meat waiting to be manipulated.

"You've been here before?"

"Yes, I used to see a girl named Jen." If she was suspicious, she gave no indication.

She dimmed the lights to a pleasant gloom. Grabbing a bottle of baby oil, she began to massage his back.

Ray relaxed. He didn't want to bring up his search for Tania until he had a chance to gauge her, and he was enjoying her hands on his body. She massaged his muscles, digging deep, squeezing, kneading. His body, relaxed but steaming. He considered the possibility that she might do something more. He looked at her, but she gave no sign either way. She started to massage his shoulders and then pounded his back muscles as if tenderizing a pork chop.

After ten minutes of deep massage, he felt her fingers ease along the inside of his thigh. Light, light touches. Very slow now. Her hands were very warm. She continued the massage, and her hand grazed his cock. Was it intentional? Accidental?

He felt the familiar urgency. Either way, the result was the same — he was heading into a tar pit of primordial instincts.

She began to lightly drag her fingers over the back of his thighs, and he felt the better part of himself come alive.

He would resist. Yes, he could. This was business, he needed to approach this professionally. He ground his pelvis into the table to keep himself from getting too aroused.

Moon continued, humming softly to herself. Soft, soft hands. Her hands felt warm, liquid gold. She continued to work, humming softly, seemingly half-present.

With a sigh, Ray propped himself up on his elbows. "Do you mind if I ask you something? Is your name Moon Li?"

Her face was a stone wall. She mumbled something. Ray sat up.

"It's OK. I just want to talk while I get my massage. My name is Ray. I'm trying to get in touch with a friend, Tania Kong."

Moon leaned back, fading into the gloom.

"Please. I work for her family. They are worried about her. Can you help me?"

He stood up. Moon backed off. A muteness about her — she was marshaling her defenses, scuttling for cover. He wrapped a towel around his waist.

"I'm hoping you can tell me a little about Tania. The last time you saw her. Do you know if she's OK?"

Her eyebrows were raised slightly, drawn inwards. Her mouth was pulled back in a small knot. Still not displaying agreement with anything he said. "How do you know my name?" she asked.

"I got your name from a friend of hers who met you once."

Moon fingered her hair absentmindedly. Her lips were pulled back tightly. "I have not seen her in over one year." Her eyes went to the floor.

"So you knew her?"

"Yes. A little."

"Do you know where she is now?"

"No." Moon's face impenetrable. Ray tried a different tack. "Moon, I know this is unusual. Can you tell me if she needs help?"

Still nothing.

"I'm not a cop. I'm not here to turn this place upside down. No one benefits." Ray leaned forward. "Can you tell me if she is OK?"

Moon stared at Ray as if searching his face for a rippling of deceit. After a time, she stirred. "I think that she's OK. I have no reason to think she's hurt. What do you want to know about her?"

Ray paused. He might as well divulge what he knew; it might put her at ease. To get information, you had to give information, and he suspected that many details of Tania's life would be known to Moon anyway.

"I did some research and found court records that showed Tania was arrested for working as a . . . courtesan."

Moon smiled. "What a nice term to describe what we do. Are you a poet?"

"Sometimes. You can only trust a poet for the first couple of lines. But I have no problem with what she was doing."

"You shouldn't. You came here," she said. "And you've been here before, right? Like you said?"

He shook his head. "First time. I came here to talk to you."

"Why?"

"To find out if you can help me get in contact with Tania. Can you help me? Her family has not heard from her in years."

"You're not a cop?"

"No. I'm a private investigator."

Moon stopped and looked him over. Then she sat down in a small chair. "Tania worked as an escort—a courtesan as you say. She worked at a private house in Chinatown."

"What kind of house?"

"Professional massage house. It was close to downtown for the businessmen. And then at night, the regulars who lived on Nob Hill."

"Were you close with her?" Ray asked. He sat down and begin to pull his clothes back on.

"Yes."

"What is she like?"

"Tania's a wonderful girl. Very sophisticated, attractive. Beautiful legs. She was one of the most popular girls in the house."

"Tell me about the house," said Ray, buttoning his shirt. Why do you ask these questions?" asked Moon.

"Her family is worried about her. No one has seen her in years. I can help her — if she needs it." Ray concentrated on keeping his dark eyes calm and flat.

Moon considered it. She explained that Tania had used the name Michelle when she worked. At the time she was reading books on alternative religions, spirituality. She defied the stereotypes of an escort: she had been well-educated overseas and invested much of her earnings in the stock market.

"She never told why she was in the life. She was smart, she could do other things. She wanted to start her own business. Some of her clients were businessmen, lawyers, athletes — famous people in the city. She used to see a famous athlete. Very famous." Moon gave an exaggerated wide-eyed look.

"Who was that?" Ray asked.

"Football player."

"Raiders or Niners?"

"Oakland," Moon nodded. "He has all these muscles. He's strong! But when he sees Tania, he's like a little sheep. He wants her to tie him up and whip his ass."

He noted the present tense: sees, wants: "She still sees the football player."

Moon gave him the stone-face. "I don't know."

"You said she was popular. In demand."

"Tania made a name for herself. She was what the clients call GFE. 'Girlfriend experience,'" said Moon sarcastically. "Like the real thing."

"Did you work with her?"

"Sometimes. We made a lot of money together."

Moon seemed to have overcame some of the inhibitions that had earlier held her back, but there was still a cold, caustic edge to her tone.

"What are most of the clients like? Good guys? Wackos?"

"Why do you think they're any different from you?" she asked.

Ray laughed. "I came here seeking enlightenment."

"Oh sure! You are all alike—horny men!" Moon laughed, enjoying the bullshit. "It's not easy. We try to fit every man's fantasy. They want to screw for five minutes. Then they want someone to listen while they complain."

"They pay you just to talk?"

"Sometimes. Men don't show their feelings, right?" she said, sarcastically drawing out the word 'feelings' like a talk show host.

Ray finished tying his shoes. "They talk about problems with their wives?" he asked.

"They're the problem. Their wives are fine. Its everything else—their jobs, their bosses. Money. Unhappiness. We're like psychotherapists."

"Except less clothing," Ray said. "But you probably get better results too."

Moon nodded. "One guy came in today and said: 'I'm ready for some poon.' Such a blunt way of getting to his needs."

"Poon, what a great word."

Silence. Moon looked more relaxed, but she still dodged the question of where Tania was living.

"Where did you last see Tania?"

"Here. She and I shared an apartment together during..." she stopped. "Before she disappeared."

Her face quivered, and her left hand whispered against her cheek.

"During what?" Ray asked.

Moon said nothing.

"You were lovers." He said it quietly, not asking a question. Her eyelids flickered slightly wider for a split second, then pulled down quickly, like shade in a private room. "For a time."

"Did you work with Tania at all during your therapy sessions?"

"Occasionally."

"Is that how you both first met?"

Moon nodded. "A client called, and asked for two Asian girls. Big deal, right? That's the most common request. The guy was a dotcom businessman. He owned some computer company in San Jose. Nice man. Lots of money and no one to share it. He rented a suite on the top floor of the Mark Hopkins. That was the first time I met Tania. I was nervous. She knew I was new to the business. She helped me, took care of me."

Ray resisted the urge to develop this scenario further.

"How often did you work together?"

"Every week after that first meeting. The guy talked about us with his friends, and we got a lot of calls. They wanted us together."

"And you were comfortable with her by this time?" said Ray.

"Very much. She looked after me."

"When did you last hear from her?"

"A while," said Moon. Her eyes were lanterns shining through half-closed shields.

"Any clients take a special interest in her?"

"They all did," said Moon. "Unlike most girls, she put her heart in it. She does that with everything."

"Anyone that you remember having some hesitation about?"

"No."

"She ever threatened by anyone? Anyone she worried about?"

Moon thought for a moment. "One guy. Not a client."

She went on to explain that, for a time, Tania resisted working long hours, and was content to be a highly paid escort who saw clients only when she desired. Her mood abruptly changed one winter afternoon.

"She was having trouble with a boyfriend. Very jealous guy." Moon picked up a towel and began scrubbing the massage table.

"Remember his name?"

"Steven."

"Last name?"

"He was Irish," said Moon, scrunching her brow. "Moore? Moran? I don't remember."

Ray took it in, showing nothing.

"You said he was jealous. How so?"

"He did not like her in the life. The strange men, the money. She was mixing with some rich people. I think he thought that she was out of his league. But that stuff never got to her. Deep down, she's a nerd; she carried around this book of poetry and read it between appointments. She was always reading."

"Did he know about you two?"

"Yes. He didn't like me," said Moon. She shifted in the chair. "He resented our friendship."

"Did Steven ever get violent with her?"

"There was some weird stuff one night. I remember that he came over one night after Tania and me got off work and had dinner together."

In his mind, Ray pictured the two of them, commuting home and washing the day's juices and dust off of each other. The world was not always deep, but it was wide.

After dinner at a Thai restaurant, Moon and Tania had returned home to find Steven waiting by the front door. He was highly flammable, vapors of rockgut wine wafting from his pores. He shouted angrily at Tania, who drew him into the confines of her bedroom. His loud shouting had continued for several minutes. He emerged fifteen minutes later, his bile neutralized by Tania's twilight softness. He left wordlessly.

"Steven faded out of the picture. I never saw him again after that night," said Moon

"What else did she say about breaking up with him? Was she involved with anyone else?" asked Ray.

"No."

"What about her interests?" Ray asked. "Dancing, clubs, yoga?"

"She was into yoga, sure. Everyone in the Bay Area does yoga." She shrugged.

"What clubs did she go to?"

"Nightclubs? She doesn't go out much. She is not a drinker."

Present tense again. He continued to admire Moon's cool beauty, so different than the Mediterranean firebrands he usually dated.

"When did you last speak with her?"

"Like I said, it's been over a year."

He looked at her face. Her brow angled low and heavy, a squall was building. The eyes just a bit tense. He was pleased—she was sensitive about this topic of her contacts. He'd gouge her a bit more.

"Moon, I appreciate you talking with me. I hope she is OK. Do you think you might in the fullness of time tell me where she is?"

"I don't know where she is." She fired a sharp smile at him.

"If you find she's in trouble, would you call me? Or tell her I can help."

Moon shook her head yes, slightly.

"Well, thanks for talking," he said. Moon looked unperturbed, yielding in defense; she was not even in the room anymore. She bent over to pick up a towel.

Looking up, Ray noticed on the mantel a photograph tucked into a frosted glass frame. The photo showed two Asian women, Moon's raw beauty dominating, Tania's lush sensuality revealing itself more gradually. Both women huddled together, windblown against a backdrop of lilac-blue sky and a smudge of golden sand. A long stretch of beach curled to the right. Orange yellow light streamed over the water.

Ray peered at the photo. "Ocean Beach or Baker?"

Moon glanced at the picture and moved to the door. "Baker," she said finally.

"If I need to talk again, how can I reach you?"

"You can find me here."

She jotted down a cell number on the back of a magazine, tore off the scrap and handed it to him. "OK, big handsome man," she said, "You come back to see me."

Ray walked down the hall to a rear exit and left the house. He felt relaxed. He strode through a path lined with reed grass and cone flowers and headed over to his car. He drove back to the hotel. The Victorians of the Haight slid by in hues of mauve, gold, aquamarine, vermilion.

Ray was pleased, especially by Moon's final comment. She had lied, but the picture was worth the thousand words she left unsaid. It often worked that way, sifting through a heap of crap until a cut diamond hit you in the forehead.

A steep cliff rose in the background of the photo on Moon's mantel. The sheer sandy wall reminded Ray instantly of Drakes Beach in Marin, a beach he knew well. Beach lore was a particular favorite of his. So Moon and Tania had once visited Drakes Beach in Marin County. But Moon had tried to hide that fact by agreeing to his suggestion that the photo had been taken at Baker Beach. The cliff at Baker was not as sheer, and the topography looked different: drifts of ice plant lined the cliffs below twisted eucalyptus trees. But why was Moon hiding the fact that she had been to Drakes Beach once with Tania? He thought about it, pictured her slight anger over his presumption that she was still in touch with Tania. Perhaps Tania was presently to be found near Drakes. Right now. And Moon knew exactly where she was.

He pulled into the garage. After he arrived back at the

hotel, he sat down to his computer and researched businesses near Drakes Beach.

Drakes Beach ran along an estuary inside Point Reyes National Seashore. The seashore hosted California's richest assortment of wildlife: coyote, bobcat, and elk were plentiful while sea lions and whales churned the ocean.

Drawn to the tremendous natural beauty, communes had sprung up in the hills near the town of Inverness. Some were headed by devout leaders steeped in ancient Eastern traditions; others were wacky California medicine shows that worshipped a Volvo-driving guru with dirty feet and a past crime spree in Florida. There were also numerous resorts catering to high-end tourists from the city. On Friday nights, fresh from their downtown offices, middle-aged corporate men arrived, comfortable in their chinoed chunkiness, recuperating for next Monday's pillage. The women, sleek and knife-haired, commanded the days behind their sunglasses, wildly overpaying for everything.

There were many resorts to check, but Ray didn't think Tania was the resort type. No, the communes seemed more promising. Like the resorts, they peppered the hills, and some were not open to the public at all. She could also be hanging out in one of the innumerable little cottages in the hills. He decided to let technology narrow the odds.

Chapter 18

In America, billions of electronic information bits were packaged for sale. Email addresses. Unpublished telephone numbers. Credit histories. A man's social security number, his wife's maiden name. Buyers abounded, both innocuous and sinister. A small industry had arisen to meet the demand, merchants of the information age, ensconced in anonymous office parks in leafy suburbs, or sequestered in decrepit buildings not quite downtown. The properties were occupied by doctors with licensing issues, lawyers with degrees from offshore diploma mills. Offices doubled as apartments, and sported doors with heavy bolts, phones answered by secretaries with cold sores that never healed. Privacy laws supposedly governed the sale of such data, but raw greed often prevailed over the niceties of federal law. In just a few years, millions of fictitious electronic golems were created, built with parts from real people—a birth date here, an address in Flagstaff, Arizona. The electronic people borrowed and spent, used credit cards. But they never actually paid a cent. In just a few years, they gummed up the world's commerce to such a degree that the financial powers gazed in worried awe at the digital morass they created, trying to keep the lid on an invisible crime spree of unprecedented proportions.

Shavonne Rabb ran her information brokerage business from a little office located inside a florist shop on Broad Street in Newark, New Jersey. She was not looking for walk-in traffic, and the locale suited her. Ray had used her successfully in the past on a few cases. She was one of the few brokers who restricted sales of personal data to the legal profession. She was sharp, discrete, quick to respond. Her voice was so soothing Ray sometimes felt like calling her just to listen to her purr. Shavonne told Ray that, with some luck, she could discover Moon Lee's cell phone and try a ruse to get her to reveal Tania's address. He asked her to get back to him within twenty-four hours.

Ray called Dominique at her office. He felt like more than business might be resolved over the next few days. After not seeing her for a few years, they were back in the routine now, seeing every other each night for dinner. It was as if they never stopped seeing each other.

"I have something for you," she said. "I got it from someone at the Bureau. For review only. No copies, if you don't mind—just read it and give it back to me. It provides some interesting background on the prostitution scene here in San Francisco." She paused. "There's a heavy Chinese criminal element involved. These are some seriously deadly people."

"I like serious people. You can reason with them."

"My concern was the deadly part. I talked to the agent about the dominant group here, the Black Fist. They have set up a drug and counterfeiting bazaar outside Naples. Working closely with the Syndicate, the Camorra. They operate factories that import huge amounts of fabric and material from China. Everything gets labeled—or relabeled— "Made in Italy" in these huge anonymous buildings north of Naples. Just acres of trash-strewn concrete. The drugs run on the same trucks as the gray market clothing.

"The Black Fist Triad has become extremely wealthy. They dominate human trafficking—prostitutes, low cost laborers, household staff for wealthy Chinese. Very dangerous people," she said.

"Come by later and we'll talk," Ray said. "I'd like to see the report."

"What about me?"

"Of course you. Especially you." They said goodbye.

Chapter 19

The cell rang. Ray stopped his pushups and hopped to the desk to pick it up.

"Ray, its Rick Perry. We've been on the subject all day. At Pier 39 now. He's leafletting. He's like a wart out there, people just move around him. With a few exceptions."

"Try to get a copy of whatever literature he's handing out."

"Will do."

"Anyone with him?" asked Ray.

"Couple of guys. Two white guys, pale, sort of goofy-looking. Classic skinhead look. Cherry has longer hair."

"The master race. Looks like this race is run."

Richard laughed.

"Let's run plate numbers on all of them," said Ray. "Are they all together?"

"More or less. They're talking occasionally. Cherry's in the middle of the boardwalk trying to chat up the foot traffic. The other two guys are hanging out nearby along a fence. One of them is throwing rocks at the sea lions. Asshole. You wonder how such a sorry-ass bunch of scabs could ever call themselves masters of anything."

Perry paused. "We had him on a different routine yesterday. He walked up Powell Street to North Beach. Near Filbert, I think it was, I'll have to check later. He stopped for a minute looking at an apartment building across the street."

Ray felt a chill. "What number?"

"1856 Powell, it's—"

"You sure?" Ray interjected.

"Yeah."

"What's the building like?"

"Three story. Mediterranean. Tile roof, lots of detail. Cherry stood across the street. Looked around for a few minutes. Could have been the building next to it but I don't think so. He was squared up. I'll find out who lives there, check the names on the mailbox."

"I know the building," Ray said. "That's my old apartment."

"No shit. I didn't know."

"What did he do after?"

"He walked over to Columbus and picked up the number 15 bus. He got off as usual at Market and headed to BART."

"Good. Good. Let's keep an eye on him on Oakland. I want an undercover in the group."

"We can manage that. It'll take some time; we have to figure out when they meet."

"Approach him at the pier—that's why the asswipe is out there, right? New recruits. Let's provide them with a recruit."

"OK, I'll get on it."

Ray hung up, walked to the bed, and lay down. He pictured the corner apartment on Powell Street, gleaming white in the western sun. The frantic activity there, the groaning bus snaking right and then left on Columbus, kids playing hoops, the thump of a soccer ball on the asphalt. Cherry leering at the carnage.

Everything blown into a million small pieces, dust filling the air on a sunlit afternoon. He would make Cherry tell him about the splinters, the cause of the dust, who was dancing because of the dust. Even if it meant pile-driving Cherry's face into concrete.

Chapter 20

A t 7:30 PM, Dominique called Ray from the house telephone line in the hotel lobby. Ray put on his coat and headed downstairs. In the lobby, he saw Dominique wearing a dark blue business suit set off with a lilac blouse and black boots. Classy. He stared just a moment longer than necessary just to let her know he was looking. She accepted the attention with a slight smile.

"Here's the notebook." She handed him a black binder titled The Triads: Origins of Chinese Gangsters. "I need it back after you're done."

"Looks good."

"According to my friend, the Black Fist has been the top group locally for many years. Street crime is split between Chinese, Mexican and black gangs. The Italians usually run their street action here through these other gangs. They're limited in San Francisco now."

"You'd never know it from Hollywood," said Ray. "They still love the Mafia. The food. The weddings."

"Watch those shows a few times?" Dominique asked.

"I like to see what stereotypes are burdening the mind of the American populace."

They headed outside the hotel. The wind whipped down Nob Hill along Sutter as pedestrians leaned into the cool air, muttering about memories of Midwestern summers. Ray told her about his visit to the massage parlor.

"Moon was intriguing. I think she knows where Tania is." He told Dominique of the photo and Moon's comment that the photo showed Baker Beach. "It's a geographical impossibility," he noted.

"You could tell that the photo was taken at Drakes?"

"I'm steeped in local beach lore."

"Didn't know tough PIs were into trivia."

"I'm in the trivia business."

They walked leisurely on Geary towards Union Square. "Moon also told me Steven Moran, the ex-boyfriend, was much more emotionally attached to Tania than he admitted to me."

"Why do you believe her?"

"I'm not sure that I do yet. I just mean that her comments about Steven were revealing, whether or not she's telling the truth. But my shit-sniffer went off the charts with her on that last comment."

"Maybe you were sniffing something else," said Dominique.

The city flowed by, cars racing from downtown, workers hauling bags of rice into a Thai restaurant. A homeless man with a silver beard lay on the gray sidewalk; shoppers cascaded by him, laden with the day's plunder.

"I feel like a steak," said Ray.

"Where do you want to eat?"

"Your choice tonight."

"I'm tired of that Tuscan olive oil stuff," said Dominique. "I want some red sauce tonight. I know a southern Italian place in North Beach that should have steak on the menu."

Cafe Etna occupied a sooty brick scar of a building that survived the twin disasters of earthquake and inferno in 1906. The owners were Sicilian, a husband and wife, both in their forties, vibrant and eternally moving, their unending industry giving intimations of major machinations behind the kitchen doors. Ray and Dominique sat down and ordered a bottle of Chianti.

He looked around the room.

"Are you OK?" Dominique asked.

"I'm fine. Why?"

"You seem distracted."

Ray said nothing.

"I've been thinking of your trip here. Seems like we never missed any time," she said.

"I know," said Ray. "I'm happy we got together."

"I hope we don't blow it again like after we graduated," she said, suddenly serious. "People seem to do that these days. I'm sorry about what happened to us. And you."

He stared into her tea-colored eyes, thinking of how the time slipped by. He had always desired her as a woman. But this topic disturbed him. They both knew why. He tried to forget the past, but rage overwhelmed any philosophy he had concocted, woven late at night, a sentence stolen from a book, a song that made sense for half a minute. But then the fury washed over him and the jetsam drifted into the darkness.

"I don't know how to move on from what happened," he said. "I'm trying." He was not sure if he was ready to discuss this with her, or with anyone.

Dominique sensed his reserve. She looked away and sipped her wine.

He put down his fork. "It's funny, the way we were. We got so involved in our jobs."

"A lot of our friends were that way," she said. "Putting in long hours. Some of them are emotional mutes. Friendships take time."

"You spend time at work with people who you have nothing in common with, other than the same person signs your check," Ray said. "All that time you miss with the people who really matter. Family, friends."

Ray looked at her. "You were always a good friend," he said. "The best of friends."

"I should have called you after it happened."

"It's OK—"

"It's not OK," she said with more feeling. "I should have been there for you."

He took her hand. "It's OK. Like I said, I didn't answer the phone for a year anyway." He looked down at his lap, tucked his napkin. "I still think of her a lot. Diana. Her name was Diana. By all odds, I should have been home with her. I had just run out for something. Tea, if you can believe it. My life, saved by a tea bag."

"I'm sure . . .." Dominique trailed off. "I don't know what to say. It's awful what happened, I'm so sorry."

"I'm glad you're here. She would have liked you."

"Thank you," she said. They sat quietly for a minute.

"I'd like to see more of you, Ray. No pressure. Nothing heavy. I know you're only here for a short time. But I'm glad we were able to see each other again."

"Me too," he said. "Seeing you again—the chance that would happen—was one of the things that brought me out here."

Dominique gave Ray a look he could not decipher. Then she leaned forward with a slight smile and looked around the room.

The waiter appeared, a young Mexican, neat and unobtrusive. A well-finessed entrance. He took their orders. Ray and Dominique watched as a customer complained about the penne being undercooked. A black-haired waiter spoke of proper cooking methods—"al dente, signori." But the lout continued to complain. Eventually, the waiter bowed to the customer's wishes and headed to the kitchen, shaking his head at the shabby tastes of American diners.

They drank wine, swirling the crimson liquid in the glass. The food came. Dominique loved the braciole, real nana's cooking—pork pounded to a thin sheet, rolled with raisins and, he guessed, mint. Ray savored an outstanding steak. One of the owners, a soft-spoken balding man, sat at the table near the kitchen, looking over at Dominique and Ray. "Next time you come, you ask me for the seafood specials—I'll make you something not on the menu. Especially for you. Just ask me." Ray shook hands with the owner. It was a good night when the chef picked you out, anointed you as one of the chosen.

The bill came and Ray reached for it, Dominique objecting mildly. They exited the restaurant and walked toward Washington Square. Saint Peter and Paul Church was lit with ground lights, sheltering the park with its grand bulk. They stood looking at the bustling street, the restaurant crowds flowing down Columbus. The scent of pines on a sea breeze, the low moan of a fog horn.

Ray took her hand and pulled her close to him. Cupping her face gently, soft skin, soft, soft. He kissed Dominique, tongue sliding over hers, lips thick and tender. He pressed against her, and she responded. They broke off wordlessly and Ray hailed a cab. One stopped and they stepped inside. Ray gave directions to Pacific Heights, and the cab headed up Union Street. The mansions of Russian Hill passed by in silence.

"Tonight I think maybe you can come up," Dominique whispered.

"I've been good," said Ray.

They were inside her apartment within ten minutes. Dominique turned on a Tiffany lamp in the hallway and Ray saw a painting with a Japanese motif of a waterfall, and an old man leaning on a staff. The hallway bore the scent of fresh-cut flowers.

"You want some wine?" Dominique asked.

"Sure."

Ray closed the door, and Dominique turned to him. They embraced in the dim light, moving sideways in some primitive crab walk, laughing as they slumped to the sofa.

"I didn't expect this," Dominique said.

"Me either. But I'm glad."

"Me too," she said. "Been a while since we were together."

"I know. Remember the water bed? The first night."

She laughed. "I felt seasick."

"You sunk into the bed. Great bounce though."

She grabbed him and squeezed.

"Still want that wine?" she asked.

"Later."

They kissed and held each other. Then a sudden impatience with buttons and zippers and the artifacts of politeness. He slipped her blouse off. Dominique's lush breasts revealed, a scent of warm skin, her nipples dark and swollen.

"Let's go to my room," she whispered. He pressed his mouth to her neck. Both breathing harder. She dug her fingers into his back as she pulled him down on top of her. Ray pushed against her, the tension powering both their bodies. He stared down at her smooth skin, her pelvic bone edged in shadow. Amber moonlight fell on the floor. Sweat evaporated in the cool night air.

The profound needs of the body. They slept deeply until morning.

Chapter 21

He woke, sunlight shining on the bed. Dominique slept soundlessly. He looked at her sunlit face. Her hair, dark and shiny on the white pillow. Lips parted slightly, like a sliced peach. She looked holy, a lost child of the sun. For a few minutes, he just watched her. He felt good. Good as he had ever felt.

He dressed quietly and she stirred. He huddled next to her, kissed her. She awoke.

"That was nice last night." She sat up and leaned her head on her elbow.

"Nice," said Ray, nodding.

"I thought it was more than nice. But that's the best I can do at this hour," she said. "Why are you awake?"

"Restless. I have a fax coming in on something at the hotel. I'm supposed to be working, remember."

"It's Saturday. Take a break, big boy."

"I did. And I will. You want breakfast?"

"I want to sleep."

"Go ahead. I wish I could stay."

She gave him an odd look, and said, "I know you have to work."

"I'm sorry. I'll call once I'm done."

Dominique smiled, crumpled her pillow, and curled into a ball, half-asleep.

"I'll call you later," he said.

Ray bounded down the creaky stairs to the street. It was just past 9:00 AM. He hailed a cab to take him back downtown to the Commodore Hotel. The morning crispness was diluted by the strong sun, and the city passed by in a lazy, offhand brilliance.

He thought about last night. He was back into it with Dominique for certain. This would be his first relationship since Diana. It felt comfortable, felt right. There was history there; they knew each other. But he felt uneasy bringing Dominique — bringing anyone — into his life right now. Given what happened, what right did he have exposing her to the underworld where he operated? He could not guarantee it was over, could not be certain some other nut wasn't waiting to engage him in some fiery afternoon vendetta. Just the other night, the thing with the guys assaulting him near the hotel. And he wasn't exactly walking away from it, not with the Project underway, the flowering of his revenge.

The cab headed down Jones Street towards downtown. As the cab pulled over, Ray watched a man walking down one side of the street towards Geary. The man looked remotely familiar — the gait, the clothes, something about him. Ray stared. As the figure turned, he recognized the face of Steven Moran. He wore a pair of enormous sunglasses. A terribly lame attempt at concealment, Ray thought — Steven looked very much like Steven, wearing huge sunglasses.

Ray directed the cab driver to turn left on Post and pull over. Steven walked slowly and peered up at the apartments; he seemed to be checking addresses or windows.

Ray paid the driver and exited. He crossed the street, and picked up a paper at a corner drug store. He pretended to scan the headlines while watching the street.

Steven Moran stood on Jones Street, his wind breaker rippling in the summer breeze. He wore baggy chinos and clumpy black shoes. Ray imagined the Tenderloin hustlers locking their teeth on this most vulnerable piece of meat: Steven's outfit screamed his lack of street smarts. He looked as conspicuous as a giraffe in rush-hour traffic, but that did not seem to bother him. Steven continued to search the facade of a blue apartment building. Ray recognized it as Tania's old residence.

Abruptly, as if some sign had been given from one of the windows above, Steven stalked up the steps and entered the building. Ray moved to a small cafe located at the opposite corner. A wood counter ran along the window; he decided he could sit there and keep an eye on the doorway. He entered, ordered a cup of tea, and took a seat next to the window. He pretended to read the San Francisco Weekly — the cover story blared about a cell of terrorists in the Bay Area who were allegedly financing their activities by producing porn films. He stared at the front of 639 Jones Street.

Ray waited for something to happen. Nothing did. No one of interest peered out the window. No one of interest exited the building. He sat there for two hours, and felt the Zen of his unceasing dedication. Then a cramped reality came back to him — he had to take a piss.

A few minutes later, the front door opened, and two Asian men exited. An eye-blink of excitement. Steven paused on the stoop, peering behind him as if waiting for others to follow. He looked nervous, frayed. The two young Asian men walked to a gray Lexus with tinted windows parked on Jones. One of them Ray recognized from the first time he had visited. The Lexus backed up into a narrow alley. Ray jumped up and tried to reestablish a line of sight. The car disappeared into the alley. Ray exited the café and walked quickly into the street, dodging traffic. He crossed the street, and saw the Lexus. A rear door was open. The door closed quickly. The Lexus pulled out into traffic and Ray looked at the plate number — K1410. Repeated the number as he ran out to the street looking for a cab.

No cab showed up for five minutes. Ray paced and stomped the pavement in frustration — the gray Lexus had faded into afternoon traffic.

Ray headed back to the café, borrowed a pen and jotted down the plate number. Then he went to the restroom and took a long-awaited piss. Outside the café, he stood for a moment, wondered if he should try to find the car. Or try the apartment again. He walked into the alley. Several metal doors opened into the building. He listened but heard no movement behind any of them. Then he walked back to the street and made his way into the apartment foyer. The doors were unlocked. He walked quietly up the stairs, and listened at the end of the hallway, peering at the room. The lights glowed weakly. There was no sound. He approached apartment 12 and knocked. No answer. Knocked again, but still no answer.

Ray walked down the hallway, and headed back to the street. He walked back to his hotel room. He stripped off his clothes and took a long, hot shower. The hot water burned his back, the pain dancing on the border of pleasure. It felt good. He thought about what he had seen: why would Steven Moran resume contact with a bunch of Asian gangbangers? He guessed that Steven had been stirred up enough by their conversation to resume trying to contact Tania. Or maybe there was another connection, something he had missed. But Steven had appeared genuinely distressed during the interview. Ray decided to run the plate, and track who owned the car. Probably stolen plates.

Another mystery to drown in. He had realized long ago he made a living chasing ghosts. Sometimes he considered leaving the profession. No more unraveling schemes. No more deciphering the truth from a thousand wayward stories, listening to grifters justify the burnt ends of their lives. He didn't want them to touch his life anymore. He'd leave this vague bullshit behind and sit in a sunny room somewhere. He'd become a painter. A rough canvas in his hands. Make things you can touch and see. Wake up at noon, give rambling interviews to slutty reporters from Art Weekly. He'd piss on a canvas, make figure eights, sell the work for six figures. Organic art. Neoclassical primitivism, with an emphasis on secretions.

He stepped out of the shower and put on dress pants and a T-shirt. He flicked on the computer, and reversed the Lexus plate; it came back to a Pacific Imports Company at 867 Stockton Street. He knew it was the address of a post office in Chinatown. Something he would check out later.

Ray took a call from Richard Perry.

"Ray, we've been on him all day. Same old song and dance. Heading to a bus stop on Bay and Columbus."

"Let's extend it," said Ray. "Follow him home today. Find out his schedule. Any luck with the undercover?"

"We're in contact. We had the undercover at the wharf yesterday."

"What's his background?"

"His name is Don Gaines. Very bright. He has an ability to get people to open up."

"Anything so far?"

"Cherry gave him some literature with a hate line, as they call it. The calls go to a recording giving the Aryan news of the day. They have a council meeting each month, but Don hasn't been able to find out where. They're careful about disclosing the location to newcomers."

"What are their numbers here in San Francisco?"

"Cherry's been talking thirties," said Richard. "I would bet it's half that."

"OK, I'll call you later." Ray ended the call.

Ray ordered room service: tea, a ham and pepper omelet, home fries and some oranges. The binder Dominique had given him lay on the table; he picked it up and skimmed it. The history of Asian crime syndicates. He flipped the pages until he came to chapter one.

"During the year 1947 AD, in the city of Hong Kong, a criminal kingpin named Chang Kong Sen organized a cadre of displaced warriors, petty thieves and other adherents to immigrate to the United States. His organization, the most powerful of the Chinese crime syndicates, and the sun around which all the others had come to orbit, was the Black Fist Triad. The Black Fist effectively controlled the city's lucrative prostitution, gambling and extortion business, known collectively as the "black society." The move to the United States perpetuated a syndicate that has existed for over 400 years.

Fact and myth have blended together, but it is agreed by most scholars that the triad origins can be traced to resistance fighters who battled the emperors of Manchuria. In the 1600s, the Manchus had invaded China from the north, sacking the Chinese capital of Peking. During the 13th year of rule by the Manchu emperor, a rebellion broke out in the province of Fukien. To lead the emperor's forces, the Manchus called upon the Sui Lan, (the name is derived from a term meaning "fighting monks"), warriors from a monastery known for its vigorous martial arts regimen. A well-trained, disciplined group of 100 warriors led the emperor's troops at Fukien, where they brutally clamped down on the rebellion. The Sui Lan were awarded imperial powers as a result of their efficient efforts on behalf of the emperor.

The Manchus grew to distrust the Sui Lan and their newfound popularity. After a few years, the Manchus made secret plans to destroy them. They laid a trap by calling upon the Sui Lan to attend a ceremony at a courtyard inside the Forbidden City. A large contingent of bowmen secretly assembled inside the city. A feast was laid out, laced with poison. The unsuspecting Sui Lan fell ill or died from the poison; those who failed to succumb were killed by carefully placed bowmen, who shot the unarmed monks as they sat in the open courtyard. Nearly all the Sui Lan monks were massacred, and the slaughter was kept secret for some time behind the walls of the Forbidden City.

However, amidst the carnage, five monks survived and escaped. In the hills far from the capital, they vowed to avenge the massacre. They founded five secret societies with names that changed frequently, often operating under benign names that suggested a commercial association. They later became known collectively as the Triads. Four Triads were eventually stamped out by Manchu troops. One survived, the Black Fist Triad, which adopted the symbol of a black fist on a field of crimson.

The Black Fist dedicated themselves to the overthrow

of the hated Manchus, whose Confucian secular lifestyle was an affront to the artistic and intellectual achievements of the Ming Dynasty, regarded as the golden age of China's cultural achievements. Although the Manchus ruled until the early 1900s, the Black Fist prospered by controlling virtually the entire Chinese black market. For the next two centuries, it expanded its power into every level of Chinese society. Historians estimate that the Black Fist had between 75,000 to 100,000 members. The Black Fist drew most of its support from the coastal cities of Hong Kong and Shanghai, where it operated those cities notorious opium dens and brothels. During World War II, the invading Japanese Army reached a secret agreement with the Black Fist, whereby the syndicate would continue to control the black society in the cities from Nanking to Hong Kong. In return, the Black Fist would provide intelligence to the Japanese regarding the nascent Communist insurgency, which was harassing the over-stretched Japanese supply lines.

Seeing an opportunity to rid themselves of a foe they saw as directly antagonistic to the black society, the Black Fist began a methodical extermination of Communists. Beginning in 1940, the Black Fist rounded up suspected Communists agents with a ruthlessness that surprised even the Japanese. Within four years, the Black Fist was responsible for the murder of nearly 10,000 Communists. Many of the murders bore signs of ritual execution, and took the form of two shots to the forehead and the back of the skull.

In 1945, the American military incinerated two Japanese cities with a devastating new weapon, the atomic bomb. Faced with the possibility of having its cities razed from the earth, the Japanese surrendered within hours of the second bombing. The Black Fist lost much of its power in the vacuum that resulted from the Japanese defeat. As the Japanese controls were thrown off, the Communists from four cities of Peking, Canton, Nanking, and Fukien surged to Hong Kong to avenge the Black Fist purges.

And the Black Fist met them. Fighting with small arms against troops armed with machine guns and rocket launchers, the Black Fist suffered enormous losses. Meeting in December 1946, the last remaining Triad bosses developed a plan to leave China and reemerge in carefully selected foreign bases. They selected five cities in which to operate, including two in the U.S.A. — New York and San Francisco.

In early 1947, the remnants of the once-powerful Triad departed mainland China. Funds had been sent abroad to ensure long-term financial health for the organization. In San Francisco, the Black Fist faction was headed by Chang Kong Sen, a 47 year old exporter who had been educated in the US before the war. Guided by Sen, the Triad began to muscle turf away from the various disorganized local gangs, extorting protection fees from small businesses and organizing a network of brothels and card parlors, often operating in hidden rooms dug into the basements of respectable Chinatown businesses. During the next two decades, they developed independent businesses in the entertainment and fashion industries, as well as finance and law. During the 1980's, the New York-Boston faction came under the control of a woman, Victoria Kong Chang, who was to become one of the Triad's legendary rulers."

Ray put the notebook down. He went to his computer and checked his email. He had a message from his friend in New Jersey — she would be faxing over a list of numbers by the afternoon. He went back to his notebook and, after lying in bed, dozed off.

He woke suddenly to a telephone call from the front desk announcing that a package had arrived. Ray went downstairs to pick it up: surveillance footage from Perry.

Back in his room, Ray drew the curtains. He always liked the room as dark as possible when he watched video. Darkness quieted the mind. He sat on the edge of the bed and slipped the DVD into the player. The digital footage appeared. In the distance he could see Bobby Cherry under the gray sky of the Bay. Seagulls wheeling, seals bellowing in the distance. Ill-dressed tourists wandered in and out of the frame, children stuffing their faces into cotton candy puffs. A performance artist he knew, the Gold Guy, doused in gold paint and standing absolutely still, tourists watching curiously. And Bobby Cherry doing his best, earnest in his efforts. He handed out literature to the crowd, talking occasionally to sympathizers, whispering code words about the white militia, the coming race wars. The secret camps were in Idaho, where you shot high-powered rifles into the mountains and kept your skin covered from the sun to glorify the paleness.

Ray paused the button occasionally, and zoomed into Bobby Cherry, looking for something in the terrain of his skull. Watching video footage was now commonplace, the novelty worn off for the youngest generations. Yet sometimes you caught someone unexpectedly, without warning. You saw the nakedness, the raw gesture. You looked for the way a man touched his chin, hidden wiring from the mind revealed in the face. Something true and real. At least you convinced yourself it was.

Ray needed to find something. He thought of her again, and heat seared his face. For the next hour, he sat in the antiseptic room, bathed in the silvery-blue light. Meditating a plan with no flaw.

Chapter 22

A s she relaxed in her apartment, Moon Lee's cell phone rang. She saw the caller ID read "County Hospital." She picked up after the first ring.

"Hello, this is the County Hospital Records Office calling for Moon Lee."

"Who is this?"

"County Hospital," a woman said. "Is this Moon Lee?"

"Yes it is. How did you get my number?"

"Are you the emergency contact for Tania Kong?"

"Oh my god, is she all right?"

"She's been in an accident."

"Oh god! — "

"She's in with the doctors now. She is OK. Before I release any more information, I need to have you confirm a few things."

"Sure, go ahead." Moon Lee reached for a pen and paper.

"Your date of birth?"

"June 9, 1984."

"Your address?"

"Haight Street San Francisco. When can I see her?"

"I'm sorry, but I don't see that address listed here."

"Why do you have to make it so difficult — "

"Can you confirm the address for Tania we have on file?"

"Yes, its Ashtanga Yoga Center in Inverness."

"OK, great."

"When can I see her? And why are you asking..."

The line went dead.

* * *

At 2:30 PM, his inbox showed the e-mail he was waiting for had arrived. Ray clicked the little envelope and opened up a scan with an address and phone number handwritten in black ink. Shavonne had gotten him what he needed.

The number was registered to a place called Ashtanga Yoga Center. It was located in Inverness, a small town near Drakes Beach. He had spent many summer afternoons there. The center was located on Juniper Road, a long highway lined with small cottages that ran by an inlet surrounded with old evergreens. It was a perfect place to hide.

Ray felt real good about the Ashtanga Center. He dialed the number. A woman's voice answered: "Hello, Ashtanga Center," hanging a question on the pause. Ray asked for directions and the woman explained that all meetings were by appointment only. He made an appointment to tour the Center later that afternoon. He dressed in tan-colored dress pants, a powder blue shirt, and then headed to the garage.

Ray took Highway 101 north through the greenery of the Presidio, an abandoned army base dotted with military officers homes, silent and stately. Fog surged over the thick steel cables of the Golden Gate Bridge as Ray crossed the bay. The bridge was a sublime creation, with soaring orange-vermilion towers that set off starkly against the straw hilltops of the Marin Headlands. All around, the Pacific roiled in blue-gray waves.

The Golden Gate Bridge was a favored spot for suicides. In the mid-1990s, the press began to report that the number of jumpers was approaching one thousand. At the 977th suicide, a bizarre countdown started, a perverse lottery for depressed Midwesterners lost in California, each one hoping to be the millennial jumper, legs flailing a death dance above the icy water. For a month, the number of jumpers surged as each suicide mustered enough self-interest to insert themselves in history as the 1000th jumper. The news media began a policy of not reporting the numbers, and the 1000th jumper leaped into a forced silence.

Ray drove beneath the painted rainbow above a tunnel entrance and approached 100 miles per hour as he cleared Marin City. He took the exit for Route 1. Past San Rafael, the lanes dwindled. He passed through hilly farms and slid off the exit, winding his way west towards Drakes Beach in Marin County.

Marin County was idyllic Northern California, a land of soaring redwoods and sheltered homes built on steep slopes, where drivers sipped six dollar lattes while wielding Land Rovers and multiple cell phones. The days burned sunny and hot, but the night air cooled precipitously. When the chill fog rolled down the hillsides, so pure and pristine, it seemed almost arctic.

The GPS system showed a confusing jumble of dotted lines surrounding Drakes Beach, a series of dirt roads winding through the pastures. Street signs would be nonexistent: the locals were notorious cranks and usually removed road signs each summer in a defiant act of isolation.

Ray headed north past Tomales Bay State Park. The bay, all windswept blues and golds, stretched off to his right, while scrub pines dotted the horizon. A stiff wind blew down from the hills. He peered into the undergrowth on his left, looking for a road into the dense greenery.

After about ten minutes, he saw a small sign posted on a tree that read simply 'Ashtanga'. He braked and headed left into the green canopy. The road ran almost straight up a hill before turning abruptly to the right and ending on a protected ridge. A stand of pine and fir obscured the road below. Above, the ridge was dense with eucalyptus and copse.

The Ashtanga Center was a two story, wooden building built in the blunt Bauhaus style, an unfortunate choice for a building that espoused a philosophy of goodwill and well-being. The fortress aspect was lessened by overflowing potted plants and stone statues that dotted the front of the building. A wooden deck extended to the west, and held several small iron tables. A few cars were parked in a small dirt clearing in front of the property.

A bell hung near the door. Ray rang and waited. The door opened presently and a woman stepped out, or glided, or projected or appeared—a granola ghost from the Age of Aquarius.

Appearing to be in her fifties, with long, gray hair, blue eyes, and fine skin crisscrossed with wrinkles, the woman smiled: "Hi! Welcome to Ashtanga. I'm Euriko Cain." She wore a turquoise robe with a cinched leather belt that fit her well. Her hands shimmered with a variety of colorful rings, bracelets, bangles. The ensemble was set off by a Navajo necklace made of mercury-colored hematite, with small figures of cut stone, cunningly fashioned into the shapes of bears, wolves, and other animals. Her entire demeanor radiated peace and goodwill, silent meals of sunflower seeds and mesquite grilled tofu. Ray thought that she probably crapped no more than twice a week.

"Hi, I'm Ray Infantino. We spoke earlier today."

Euriko smiled, and guided him into a foyer enclosed on three sides with sliding glass doors. Soft music played, a sitar's eastern jangle. Beyond the doors, he could see a courtyard decorated with jade plants and carefully trimmed bonsai. A number of people clad in simple garb were stretching in the courtyard. Ray smelled the sweet scent of jasmine. The entire place was imbued with a peaceful simplicity that made native New Yorkers feel like they were on Neptune.

Euriko fluttered about, talking earnestly about herbal tea curing the horrors caused by America's wretched affair with the coffee bean.

"Coffee has a toxic effect on the internal organs. It's poisoning this country. It is a dangerous drug and has destroyed more people than alcohol. Coffee caused the fall of the Incas."

"At least they were awake when it happened," said Ray. "But I thought Pizzaro caused the fall of the Incas."

"No, he killed the Mexicans." Ray decided arguing with

her might dent her well-being and so he kept silent. She smiled and walked him toward a double door. "Have you been to a yoga center before?"

"No, I haven't. But they offer yoga at my gym. I picked up a few poses here and there."

Euriko sniffed a potential convert. As they walked through the center, she managed to reference the names of various distinct and foreign disciplines including crystals, aromatherapy, pyramids, feng shui, Tarot, colonics, and nude yoga.

"All these combine in our color wheel of healing modalities. You should try a few classes." Ray walked on, nodding politely at the blahblahblah. Still, he liked her.

As they strode through the complex, various people walked by, nodding briefly but mostly keeping a calm, detached manner.

Euriko guided Ray to the main yoga studio, a room with mirrored walls, heated to a toasty 90 degrees, and populated by ten barefoot people stretching their backsides towards heaven.

"A fitting pose: the nexus of heaven and earth."

"I beg your pardon," Euriko asked.

"That pose, downward dog."

"You are familiar with the poses! How nice."

"Is the center open to the public?" Ray asked.

"Well, a certain section is open to the public, but the majority of the center is reserved to private study. The center houses serious devotees of yoga practice who work here in various ways to support the center. You would need to apply."

"I may be interested in such an arrangement. Do you have time to show me the rest of the center?"

"Sure." Euriko floated away from the studio. "I didn't realize you were considering such a big commitment."

Euriko walked him to a locked steel door that read *Residents only please.* She opened the door with a key, and gestured for Ray to enter. A long hallway stretched in front of him, with various doors opening up on both sides. The decor was Spartan, mostly black and white pictures of nature scenes, a few aloe plants or cut flowers in vases on stone pedestals. He noticed the sound of bubbling water coming from somewhere, picked up the scent of lavender. He breathed deeply; it really was relaxing here.

They walked down the orchid-colored corridor, and Ray saw Tania walking right toward him.

For a second, his mind refused to comprehend the face for which he had been searching, now physically present, right in front of him. The thoughtfulness of her eyes struck him, and a cool thrill ran through his gut. She walked with the firm, elegant movements of someone comfortable with her body, her legs balanced and poised. She was attractive, the face tan and well-formed. Her hair was long, longer than he remembered from the picture, and her mouth was unusual, shot through with a puffiness to the lips that lent her a tough, almost cruel, aspect.

Ray looked at her as she approached. She was carrying a laundry basket. She glanced at him, and moved on without smiling.

Ray walked with Euriko for a few more paces, hardly listening. Then he stopped.

"I think I know her. Tania, right?" he said softly, gesturing to Tania as she disappeared around the corner in the hallway.

"You know her?" Euriko asked.

"I've been in touch with her family. Do you mind if I speak with her?"

Euriko touched her hair with a finger, looking concerned. Ray started to walk back down the hallway. She then stepped quickly in front of him. "Please wait here. Let me check with her first."

Euriko walked back to the hallway, calling quietly for Tania. Ray waited, not sure if she would be spooked.

After a minute, Euriko returned, looking suspiciously at Ray. "She'll see you in the courtyard, follow me." Her

New Age sweetness was evaporating. Ray kept up a benign cheerfulness.

They walked down a hallway. Euriko opened a wooden door on her left. She and Ray stepped out to a brick courtyard with a small pool and several chairs. Tania huddled outside in a courtyard on a crude wooden bench. She looked up as Ray approached and he saw fear break the surface of her dark eyes. Her eyelids were sharply pinned and her mouth bent into a slight frown.

Euriko hovered near the doorway, while another center denizen, a bearded, skinny man, stood nearby, absentmindedly holding a shovel. Ray sat down next to Tania, careful to keep his distance.

"Tania, my name is Ray Infantino. I'm an investigator. A lawyer for your family retained me. They're concerned about you. They wanted to find out if you're OK."

"My family? Who?" she asked, covering her mouth with a cupped palm. "How did you find me?"

"I did some research, talked to some people," he shrugged.

She sat still, assessing him. She touched her nose absentmindedly. He started again, keeping his voice level deep, reassuring. No sudden gestures. He tried to gauge the reasons behind her fear.

"A lawyer named Lucas Michaels hired me after you lost contact with your family a few years go. They're concerned about you, Tania."

She stared at him in a penetrating silence. Her brows were slightly drawn in, her eyes wide.

"He told me about your family. About your father." Her eyes shut briefly. "I knew you had once lived in California. Are you interested in getting in touch with your family?"

Tania looked down. "Who exactly? I mean—I'm sorry, this is a shock. That anyone could find me so easily." She picked absentmindedly at a fingernail.

Euriko called over, "Are you all right Tania?"

"I'm fine," she said, glancing quickly over her shoulder.

She looked at Ray. "So much has happened."

"How did you end up here?" asked Ray.

"I was—you didn't tell me how you found me." Her hands pressed into her thighs.

"I'm an investigator. Among other things, I locate and interview people for a living. Databases, phone records." Ray shrugged. "It's a minimal requirement for the profession."

"Can anyone get that information?" Tania asked.

"Not easily. Most investigators only get this information for clients they know well. But I have to admit, I was lucky with you. So no, you otherwise would not have been easy to find. Quite the opposite, in fact."

He paused. "You seem worried about being found here. Are you having problems with someone?"

Tania looked away, a mute wall of confusion. Ray could see his words were just bouncing and clanking off a layer of invisible armor. They sat silently, Tania staring bleakly at the red brick patio.

At last she looked up. "How did this lawyer hire you?"

"A referral. We know some of the same attorneys in Boston." Tania shifted her weight, rocking slightly, but said nothing.

"Your family is worried about you. Tania, I didn't mean to upset you by coming to see you. Your family thinks that you might be in some kind of trouble. They want to help. I can help. But you have to tell me what's going on, why you're here."

"A lot of things have happened. And now you, out of the sky." Tania put her left hand over her eyes. "I need to think. Need time."

Some witnesses could be maddeningly evasive, he knew, especially Asian witnesses. They wouldn't argue or fight; they'd just wait you out, turn the conversation into something slippery and angular. He admired the tactic. Just as water eventually ruts stone, they won in the end.

"What would you like to do?" Ray asked.

"I need time. I have some decisions to make. Please don't tell the lawyer you found me. Not yet."

She had locked in on his dilemma. His task was accomplished, it was over, should he define it as he ought. He should call Lucas now, and inform him of her location. Await further instructions. That was what he had been hired to do. But he needed to find out more. There was an undercurrent of fear running through this woman. That was unexpected. He worried that she might flee. But he could take precautions.

"I can't agree to not tell my client."

"Why?" Tania asked.

"He paid me to find you. It's not ethical to keep it from him."

"Well, I won't be able to be meeting anyone yet." She looked away, her mouth knotted, eyes bright.

"It's your decision about whether you want to contact him. He knows that."

"Will you at least agree to hold off until morning?" Tania asked.

"I'm open to that possibility if you agree to meet again early tomorrow," said Ray.

She put her hands together like she was praying. "OK."

"We'll talk more in the morning." He stared at her, tried to get some glimmer into her mindset. But she averted her face.

"Thank you." Tania got up abruptly and led Ray to a faded red door leading out of the courtyard. She opened the door, and stepped into the receiving room where he had been earlier. The jasmine incense wafted through the doorway. Tania said a faint goodbye, turned, and headed back out the red door. Ray watched her go, her thin frame graceful but flickery; she looked like a cornered animal, backed into an alley and ready to lash out in a desperate and unexpected way.

Euriko stood with feet apart, watching Ray. "So you were not really interested in yoga after all." Her face looked gray now.

"Actually I am," he said. "I really do like your studio." Offering only a remnant of goodwill, Euriko showed him to the door. He felt like he had disappointed a minor deity.

"I'll be meeting with Tania tomorrow."

"That's fine." Euriko forced a quick smile. The door shut and Ray walked back to his car.

He slowly drove off beneath the canopy of firs and pine, and headed toward the main road. After driving down the road for a quarter mile, he turned off into a dense stand of pines. He pulled close to a clump of branches so that his car was obscured from the road. Then he sat back in his seat and watched the road to the Ashtanga Center.

Chapter 23

R ay suspected that Tania might try to sneak away from the center during the night. She was petrified, clearly under duress. Surveillance would be necessary. There would be the usual problems. If a car drove down from the hill at night, identifying the occupants would be difficult. She could scramble through the woods at midnight — the place teemed with insects, snakes, even cougars — and try to reach one of the hiking trails that ran near the property. He had to put someone on the hillside, humping the bushes.

By 7:40 PM, the sun dropped its scarlet robes and faded into a gray Pacific slumber. A wind blew in from the ocean. Birdsongs whistled from the pines and then fell silent. He waited beneath the trees, vigilant, relaxed. After a few minutes, he called Richard Perry; yes, Perry could send four guys out there immediately. Ray told him he had a special assignment: he needed at least one guy with some woodcraft, keeping track of some walking trails at night. Richard said that his crew could handle the job with no problem — four men would be at his disposal within two hours.

As night deepened, Ray heard several cars approaching. The surveillance team arrived: three cars slithered into the pines and parked near Ray's vehicle. He put his parking lights on to illuminate the clearing. In the gloom, Ray watched the men assemble, dressed in jeans and sneakers. They were fleshy, sardonic, always looking for a joke. A pie-in-the-face type of crew. Three looked alert and sharp-eyed. One looked slack and heavyset, and spoke in an overly familiar way. Ray decided immediately that he didn't want that clod crawling through the underbrush. He decided to place two of the three aces — Joe Ronaldino and Art Hulme — on the hillside trails. They had specialized in stakeouts throughout rural San Diego county while working for the DEA, and were equipped with night vision goggles. All had two-way radios, and could be in touch with anyone of the others at a moment's notice. Ray reached into his file and passed around the photos of Tania. The men began to get ready to hike up the hill.

"Don't let the bears scare you," said Ray.

"That's what this is for," Ronaldino said, pulling out a Desert Eagle semiautomatic pistol.

"Overkill! You could down a rhino with that fucking thing."

He directed the two other operatives to fan out at various points at either side of the road so that both directions would be covered.

Fog rolled over the ridge, nestling in the valleys and muffling sound under a thick grayness. Ray sat in the car past midnight and watched the dark road. They exchanged a few calls every hour — no one had left the center.

A sunless morning arrived. His legs were cramped and his muscles urged him outside. He directed a refreshing piss into the pine needles. Everyone would be hungry. He drove to a small roadside store and picked up some pastries, muffins and coffee. Back at the pine knoll, he called and had each investigator walk down alone. They sipped coffee and made small talk among the pines.

Ray spoke to Hulme, who did some ursine grunting as he stretched his shoulder muscles. "Let's keep this going up on the hillside, at least until noon. I should know by then if we continue."

All right. How about the other three?"

"They can go. I'm going up there soon, and between the two of us, we should be able to track her if she makes a run."

Ray was jumpy now, amped up with sugar and distorted hours. After a few minutes, engines rumbled to life and the other three operatives headed back to San Francisco. Hulme walked across the street and headed toward the walking trail. He disappeared into the woods.

Ray sat in the car, watching a hawk spiral above the

highlands. A subtle symphony of morning sounds, bird cries, fluttering wings, rose from the meadows. Remarkable after being in the city where the buses roared, horns honked, voices chattered—all that modern buzz missing amid the green of Tomales Bay.

Ray washed up as best he could with bottled water and some paper towels. Just after 9:00 AM, he heard the sound of a chugging motor. A car drove up the highway. Within moments a gray Honda roared by and slowed as it prepared to turn into the Ashtanga driveway. Inside the car, Ray saw long black hair framing a familiar, well-formed profile. He smiled.

Moon disappeared up the driveway, her car swallowed by the fog.

Ray paused. He heard another car coming. A black Mercedes raced along the road. Tinted windows, custom wheels of glittery platinum. The car slowed and prepared to turn left into the Ashtanga roadway.

Through the front windshield, Ray could dimly see the interior of the car. It bristled with men, shoulders jammed tight together. The car shot up the hill. A warning went off in his reptilian brain—these men weren't here for the morning yoga class.

Ray started his car and tapped his fingers absently on his shoulder holster. The reassurance of the Beretta semiautomatic. He aimed the car across the highway and raced up the road to the center. The car shuddered as he took a sharp right halfway up the hill.

He grabbed his phone and hit the direct connect to Hulme: "We got visitors. The girl in the Honda I know, the Mercedes looks like trouble."

Hulme came back, heavy static—"Hear you, Ray! I'm above the center now."

"Where?"

"Straight ahead, just above the path. Before you turn right into the lot."

Up ahead, the Ashtanga Center lay shrouded in the early morning silence of the mountain. Everything looked damply green, except the two cars on the unpaved lot, which looked alien and unwelcome. The Mercedes had stopped at an odd angle. He saw Moon standing on the front landing. She stood with one hand on the door knob, looking back hesitatingly at some unheard command issuing from the Mercedes. She paused, fear drawing her face in; she started to back away. The Mercedes vomited several Asian men in dark clothes. Two men moved quickly to the porch. One gesticulated harshly and pulled out a pistol.

The men looked over as Ray's car advanced up the street. They reached for jacket pockets. One man wore a slightly mad grin.

Ray felt his nerves spark with an adrenal rush, elemental colors emerging from grays, sounds shedding their mufflers. He drove towards the building, quickly preparing for a private little war in the hills.

A commotion behind the men in the center — female voices rising, a minor panic in the new-age woods. For a moment, the men seem undecided.

Ray never stopped the car. Racing the engine, he headed to the right of the center. He drove straight past the Mercedes and bounced over a raised garden bed, wheels churning through bok choy and cabbage. The tires sunk into the damp ground, spinning ineffectively before propelling him toward a flagstone patio behind the complex. He raced over the bumpy ground and thudded onto the stone. He drove for a hundred yards or so, feeling the wheels slip over the dewy stone. He screeched to a halt near the rear of the complex. Maybe one hundred-fifty yards from the men in front, he guessed. He had little time.

He leaned out the window and shouted for Tania, glancing at five doors that he guessed opened into the courtyard where she had been yesterday. He had no idea which door opened to her room.

One of the middle doors opened. Tania's sleep-creased face peered out. The growing mayhem, angry voices barking at the front of the complex. Ray, his car weirdly out of place on the patio. She looked back into her room and then darted out, racing across the patio. She ran for the woods.

Ray shouted at her again. She heard gunfire at the front, voices shouting. Some of the shots sounded like they were coming off the ridge.

Tania hesitated. Ray was frantically waving her on, looking back to the front of the property. His eyes were big, intense. Then Tania angled back to Ray's car, running hard. He opened the door. He started to back up even as she closed the door.

Around the corner of the building, she saw two Asian men materialize, breathing hard, faces gaunt. Hands lifted dark-colored guns.

Ray drove right at them in reverse, engine revving.

"Look out!" she shouted.

The car bobbed over the rough ground. Then a meaty thump—the car smashed its way over one of the men. Dirt sprayed wildly from the tires. The car cleared the pile of cracked bones. "Oh god, you hit him, you hit him!" she yelled. The heavy thwack of something heavy hitting metal echoed in her brain. Things not meant to touch at high speed. She felt a little sick.

Another man ran toward them, pointing a gun. Ray slowed and turned the car around. He raised his Beretta and blasted three rounds at the man, who twisted away from the car and fumbled his weapon. Cracks reverberated off the rocky hillside. The man cried out, sagged and twisted to his knees and pressed his hands into his thigh. The burning smell of cordite suffused the cramped interior.

Ray wasn't sure how many men were out front. But no where else to go. He gunned the engine again. To his right, he saw the yoga center reeling by like a movie he had watched in another life.

The demolished garden came into view. An Asian man stepped out quickly from the corner of the building, aiming his gun. As the car careened at him, his eyes swelled wide. He dove right, firing wildly into the damp soil. More shots and the right rear window cracked. A sour burning smell. "Keep your head down!" Ray yelled. Tania crunched herself almost flat on the seat.

The car drove off the raised bed and thunked into the pavement near the front of the house. Two men raced after him and fired wildly. Ray spun the car left in the driveway. The centrifugal forces dispelled, and he was facing downhill. Then the air around him crackled and smoked. He jammed the car in gear.

More gunfire. One Asian man stumbled, his upper torso jerking awkwardly like a shattered puppet—Hulme had picked him off from the hillside. Hulme continued to fire in staccato bursts, confusing the men below. They looked harried and frayed now, peering into the hills for shooters they had not expected. So many shots, there had to be more than one sniper. This fight was not for them. The knife across a throat; a close-range shot inside a dark nightclub—that was their game. Out here they were lost, firing blindly into the shadowy evergreens.

Ray winged forward and jammed a hard left. The car dipped down the gully. He guessed that they were now out of the sight line of the building. Accelerated down the incline, braking hard as he approached the main road. He considered turning left and heading towards Bodega Bay, but he was not familiar with the way—better to be certain of where he was going. He turned right. The Mercedes was nowhere in sight.

The Asian crew had lost the element of surprise. He thought about backtracking to make sure Hulme was safe, but he thought the gangbangers would break off now that Tania was gone. Hulme was just a deadly presence in the woods, they weren't about to chase him. Tania was the target.

Ray dripped with nervous energy. Tania twisted back to

peer over her shoulder, watching the road behind them.

"What happened? Who are these guys?" she said.

"I think they followed Moon here."

"Moon! She's here!' Tania's face was ashen. "We have to go back!"

"No way! They don't care about her—if they did why follow her all the way from San Francisco."

"She could be killed!"

"If they wanted to kill her, she'd already be dead. They want you, not her."

Tania slumped to the seat, saying nothing as she buried her face in her hands.

Ray drove eighty miles per hour; even though he saw no pursuit, he wanted to head for civilization, be near witnesses, near something. He felt exposed on the empty country roads. Ray dialed Hulme on his cell phone.

"Art, are you OK?

"I'm OK. You?"

"OK. What's happening there?" He watched the rearview mirror for signs of pursuit.

"They're gone," said Hulme. "She was the target. Lots of cops here now. I'm talking to a detective now. They want to talk to you—"

"OK, tell them I'll call later. Emergency." Ray hung up. His phone rang right away but he ignored it. He would deal with law enforcement later. Right now, this was a private matter.

He got on 101 and drove straight to the city. After cruising for thirty minutes, he eased up: traffic was thickening and high speeds were no longer possible. The sun was beginning to slice the fog into wispy gray ribbons.

He and Tania didn't exchange a word. Lucas would be pleased: he not only had located Tania, she was sitting in his car.

JOHN F. NARDIZZI

Chapter 24

The Golden Gate Bridge ended in a spread of toll booths. They drove through the tall pines and eucalyptus of the Presidio, past the Palace of Fine Arts, up Lombard to Van Ness. He turned up several narrow streets, winding circuitously up Russian Hill. At last he stopped on Filbert Street overlooking San Francisco Bay. To his left was the Golden Gate Bridge. To his right, Alcatraz Island jutted amid the green waters, forlornly beautiful as its sun-bleached prison walls crumbled in the salt air.

Ray drove on. He replayed the sickening collision, the pointblank shots. He wondered if both men were dead. He knew he should feel something, but for now, those men were like mushrooms beneath his feet. His body was shunting off all emotion into his survival instinct. He turned and bore all his energy into Tania.

"We need to talk details. Now. Talk about who you're hiding from. If you want help, you need to tell me."

"Who are you?" she hissed.

"I told you. Your family hired me through their attorney." Tania sat staring at him.

"Look, whoever that was back there, I'm obviously not with them. So that's a start. Other people besides me were able to track you to Marin. Who are you hiding from?"

Tania sat curled-up and looking small. After a pause, she looked up. "I'm not sure specifically who they were, their names. But I think they're triad members."

"Which one?"

"Black Fist."

"Why are they looking for you?"

Tania cupped her hand to her mouth and paused. "I saw something I wasn't supposed to see."

"So you're a witness. To what exactly?"

"The murder of a businessman. He was killed in a gang dispute a few weeks back."

Ray looked around. This section of Russian Hill was peaceful and secluded. He decided that they would stay put for now.

"How did it happen?"

"I was in the room with him," said Tania. "Right before they came in and did it." Ray watched her. She still looked dazed.

"Did it involve your job?" he said quietly. She hesitated. "I saw the arrest in 1997."

"Yes." She frowned a little. "A date was arranged. He took two of us to a hotel on Mason Street. He wanted two girls. A two-girl fantasy. After we were done, he went outside to smoke a cigarette on the balcony. The other girl, Cindy, went out there with him."

"What hotel?"

"The Senator. Near Taylor."

"OK. Go on."

"Well, she took him out there and they had a cigarette. It was raining a little. I sat back on the bed, getting dressed. There was a breeze coming from the window. I remember Cindy laughing and smoking. Outside with the man." Tania paused, rubbed her temples, and then resumed.

"At one point, she came in, and then locked the door after her. I thought she was joking—I didn't understand why she would do that, locking the door. I could see him behind the small window in the door, his silhouette. He was leaning over the balcony, looking down at something."

"Who was he, what was his name?"

"Johnny Cho." Tania brushed her hair back and looked down at her legs. "Cindy was trying to get her stuff together but she was nervous. There was a commotion on the fire escape. Johnny was trying to get in. He was shaking the door but he couldn't open it. I didn't really understand what was going on. There was a scuffle and then I heard gunshots. There were men on the balcony. They were trying to get in the room. I ran down the hallway. There was another man waiting. He had something covering his face, like a bandanna. He shot Cindy in the back as she ran. I heard her cry out and fall behind me. I kept running. It went crazy then. Everyone was in the hallway. All these people running around, half-dressed. The man shot at the ceiling, and yelled for everyone to get down, but it was total panic. The owner came running upstairs with a gun. We ran back and forth, everyone screaming and shouting. There was a lot of gunfire and a guy in the hallway was hit pretty bad. The other guys escaped. Cops were all over the place a few minutes later."

"So there was a police response."

"Yes. A lot of people were hurt that night. The story was all over the news. Vans and lights, reporters trying to get comments from people."

Ray glanced out the window. An old lady walked her dog on the sidewalk. "What did you do next?" Ray asked.

I left. No one had any record of me being in the room. The place was rented by the client. He probably signed me in with whatever name he felt like. A cop stopped me and took me to the station. And they were watching me. Saw me get in the car." She sighed. "In our world, snitching is a death penalty. Even though I never said anything, they would never believe it. Eventually I got out and headed to Moon's house."

"How did you know Moon?"

Tania looked straight ahead. She rubbed the back of her left hand vigorously. "It's complicated. Moon and I worked at a house run by the Triad."

"A massage parlor?"

"Yes."

"You worked with her at the parlor?"

"Yes. They ran it, kept the place secure, handled the money."

"Where did they find the women who worked there?"

"Everywhere." Tania looked irritated at the question.

"Finding girls is never a problem. The girls are there for lots of reasons. Families to feed back home. Debts. Other reasons. There is no one reason."

"Are some forced to work?"

She shrugged. "Not really forced." She looked out the window. Ray could see she did not want to answer too many questions about her former profession.

"How did you get involved?" Ray asked.

"I was—" She trailed off. "My father was a member of the triad. He married into another triad family. Our families were close."

"Who did he marry?" Ray asked.

Victoria Chang. When my father died, she turned me out. Then she sold everything he had."

Victoria Chang had been identified as the head of the Boston syndicate. "Chang was your mother?"

"She's not my real mother." Tania looked down at her feet. "She married my father."

Seeing her distress, he stopped pushing in that direction. "Anyway, you were at Moon's house. What happened then?"

"I got to Moon's, and we stayed up all night talking until I fell asleep. The next morning, I looked at the paper. There was an article about the killings. I saw the names of the victims at the hotel. One was the client, Johnny, who hired us. He turned out to be a local boss. But the other name was a Black Fist soldier, Lee Fong. They ran a photo—he was arrested before, I guess. I knew him. I had seen him before at one of the houses. People said he did protection work for the triad."

"Why would a Black Fist soldier shoot Cindy?" Ray asked.

"The police said the killings were related to a turf war. But I knew that wasn't the full story. We were witnesses to the shooting. But I saw Cindy lock Johnny Cho outside on the balcony. So she was part of the plan. And then she was killed. I was supposed to be next. Because who can trust two whores who witnessed a murder? Who really cares if we turn up dead?"

She stopped talking and looked out the window.

"And it made sense. I worked off most of my debt, and so I was not worth much to them anymore."

"What debt?"

She said nothing.

Ray checked outside again but no one was around. He rolled down a window. "Where did you go after you figured all this out?"

"I stayed with Moon for a few hours. No one knew about us, I was pretty sure. I left late that night and hid out in a club. A few weeks passed and everything seemed like it had died down. Until yesterday."

Ray looked at her. Parts of her story bothered him. "Weren't you worried about staying in the Bay Area? You're only seventy miles from San Francisco?"

"Of course I was worried. But this is my home. Where else could I go?" Her forehead lined with worry. "And I was worried about Moon," she said. "Do you think they followed her to Marin?"

"I think so. After she pulled into the Center, I saw a black Mercedes come up right behind her. I assume they followed her from the city. How they managed to lock in on her I'm not sure. Maybe they followed me to her the previous day. Although I doubt it."

They sat for a while.

"What do we do?" she asked.

"Let's get indoors for a while. I need to speak to my client later today."

Tania brushed her hair out of her eyes. "Wait. That is something I need to ask you about. Can you tell me again how this lawyer is involved?"

"He called me," Ray said. "He was referred by a mutual friend. We'd run across each other before. He told me your family — specifically your sister — had retained him. She is worried about you."

"My sister? I haven't spoken with her for two years. I was

afraid they might find me through her. They used her before."

"How?"

She looked down and said nothing.

Ray sat back and thought about his first meeting with Lucas.

"I kept your confidences — against my better judgment — for a short time. But remember, I owe a duty to report back to my client. At this point, I have to at least tell him I found you. But we won't arrange a meeting until you decide how you want things to go. Plus, I need to research a few things."

She nodded.

"We need to get to some place safe."

Ray pulled away from the curb and headed east past whitewashed apartment buildings that lined the steep streets of Russian Hill. He raced down Union Street, timing the lights, and darted into North Beach. He turned left toward the Wharf, then turned up Filbert Street onto the slope of Telegraph Hill.

Telegraph Hill had a glorious, tottering beauty about it, defiant in the face of inevitable earthquakes. The hill commanded views of the Golden Gate Bridge, Alcatraz and Angel Island. Originally called Loma Alta, the precipitous hill had been home to roughhouse sailors and immigrants in the 1800s. Later, artists and bohemians moved in, attracted by spectacular views and cheap homemade wine served in North Beach restaurants. The neighborhood had long been gentrified by professionals. They drove German sedans, bought organic fruits, and overpaid for eight hundred square foot condos with original molding. But the neighborhood was still flecked with oddballs who had managed to thrive in the sharply angled neighborhood, the local cafe owner or a Chinese family who resisted the upwardly mobile erosion.

Ray stopped at Union and Kearny. Halfway down Kearny, he turned left into a driveway. He looked around — no one in the street, no one tailing.

He pulled up to a Spanish Revival home with a red stucco

facade. A rotted balcony ran along the second floor. One of Ray's oldest friends, Antonio Flores, lived there. They had grown up together in New York. Antonio taxed friendships. He disappeared for weeks at a time, and then showed up at friends houses unannounced, past midnight. He was blunt to the point of crudity, but Ray forgave it as an occasional antidote to California dopiness. Antonio's loyalty was canine, so Ray didn't feel hesitant in knocking on his door unexpectedly.

Ray knocked and heard a heavy braying of dogs. A squat rawboned figure abruptly opened the door. He had Doberman-thick black hair and a superbly scarred face, so prehistoric that it looked as if he had murdered his way from the Gold Rush era into modern times.

"Ray! God, come on in!" Antonio motioned for them to enter. He looked at Tania and smiled deeply, extending a hand. Ray looked at Tania, who appeared bedraggled and almost out on her feet. He did not waste any time.

"Antonio, I'm in a bind. She needs to disappear for a while. We had trouble this morning in Marin."

"You're family Ray, you know that. Whatever you need."

"Tania, do you need anything? A drink?"

She nodded.

Antonio motioned them inside. He was wearing black shorts with yellow neon trim and a black shirt with sandals.

"Can I make a call?" Ray asked.

"Phone is in the living—hell, you know where everything is! Let me get you something to drink."

Ray headed into the living room, where a menagerie of stuffed animal heads—zebra, bear, lion—peered silently from the pine walls. Rustic pine furniture and an enormous television. Ray sat down beneath a wolf's head, and collected his thoughts. Then he dialed Lucas.

"We had trouble today. As I told you, I tried to meet Tania last night. The meeting went well. But she's running from a group she was involved with. An Asian gang. A group of them surprised us in Marin this morning. Rough going, but we got out of there."

"How is she?" Lucas interrupted.

"She's OK. Exhausted at this point."

"Where is she?"

"At a friend's."

"Where is that?"

Ray sensed the urgency in Lucas's voice. "Trust me when I say she is in a safe place. I don't want to say too much— I am sure you understand. I can confirm it later with you."

Lucas paused. "Yes. Yes, I understand When can I see her? We need to set a meeting."

"Can you fly out?"

"I can fly out tonight, if you want. Where should we meet?"

"I'll email you a place in a few hours."

"OK. Great work today, Ray."

"I'll be in touch with the time and place."

Ray called and checked his messages at the office. Nothing urgent. He hung up the phone. He walked over a floor laid with Mexican tile to the living room. Tania sat there on a sofa, sipping a large glass of orange juice, her hair neatly combed. Antonio looked like a freshly groomed dog at a show, leg wiggling in suppressed excitement. Tania's Asiatic elegance was having its way with him. Antonio was bragging about his exploits as an amateur panner who, each September, traveled to the Sierra Nevada Mountains to pan for gold in the cold mountain rivers. He hid his small findings of gold throughout the house, mixing the gold flecks with sand in empty baby food jars. His gleanings to date amounted to no more than twenty ounces of gold, but he was in it for the long haul. He wasn't starving though; he owned several rental properties in the city. He was retelling a story that he repeated at any gathering of friends: "I told the adjuster, if you stay on my property, I will be forced to discharge a firearm in your general direction."

"Antonio, enough gun talk. We've had enough guns discharged at us already."

"Sorry. What the hell happened to you today?"

"It's a long story." Ray recounted the fire fight in the woods.

"Unreal," said Antonio. "You can stay here a while." He turned to Tania. "So how do you feel being with a famous detective?"

"Watch it," Ray said. "I'll slap you six miles south of stupid."

"You can't move granite, baby."

Ray and Antonio bantered while Tania sat and read a magazine, taking in the carom shots. Ray thought Tania was finally beginning to relax a little; Antonio's attentive energy seemed to boost her spirits. At least as far as it went. He hadn't discussed it with her, but he was concerned about the firepower they would face — these were people who, after all, had shown a belief that resolution flowed from muzzle of a gun.

"Antonio, Tania and I need to talk a bit in private. Can we sit outside on the back patio?"

He laughed. "Sure, just toss me out of my own home. I'm heading out anyway. I'll be back later. Make yourself at home." Antonio walked into another room, where they heard him rummaging in a closet.

Tania was hungry, but exhaustion was braying louder. She slumped into a rocking chair and closed her eyes.

"Ray, before we talk, I need to lay down and rest."

"OK."

He walked her to one of the rear bedrooms. The shades were drawn and the room was dark and cool.

"This is a guest room. You'll be fine here."

Tania lay down on the bed without a word.

Chapter 25

Ray picked up the phone and called a back line at the Berkeley offices of the Southern Law Project. A familiar voice answered, his old roommate Kevin Burgess. They made arrangements to meet later that afternoon at the Embarcadero Cafe.

Seabirds whirled overhead. They ordered coffee and watched the massive freighters ease their way toward the Oakland waterfront.

"Anything new with the Bobby Cherry investigation?"

"Nothing new, Ray." Kevin squinted behind his glasses. He wore one of his dozen navy blue suits, an item that seemed to reproduce in the darkness of his closet.

Kevin began to recount the details in a staccato delivery. "We check on him every few weeks. Still lives in Oakland. Holding a job. Not that active as far as we can tell. Tries to get some recruiting activity going along the Oakland waterfront, which as you know is the main port in the area. No one's buying what he's selling. Mostly black workers there anyway. He passes leaflets to the white guys and talks to them about the coming race war. He's a dipshit— they usually chase him home."

"Any sight of Cherry with other members?"

"No, but—"

"I still think that he's tied in," Ray interrupted. "More than we think." He was disappointed that the Center had not developed more information. Cherry had been seen in the area before the bombing and was questioned by police. But everything had stalled since the initial frenzy of work.

Ray knew that Kevin was doing everything he could on the Cherry case. He had busted his brain studying, one of the hardest-working students Ray had known. After graduating from law school, he began working for a pitiful salary at the

Southern Law Project. Over the next few years, he developed the legal stratagem that led to a massive civil judgment against a local Aryan Knights group, effectively bankrupting the organization. An appreciative local attorney nicknamed him 'Ka-ching Kevin' – no attorney had ever been as successful at flipping the coat pockets of the Aryan Knights.

Kevin sat quietly, sipping his coffee. "We're doing all we can with limited resources, Ray."

"I know," Ray said. He took a deep breath.

The two men sat in the sun. A group of tourists were pointing at a group of California sea lions that were baking their hides on a wooden dock. Two guys tossed rocks near the dock.

"How often do you get him under surveillance?"

"At this point, we just get reports on him from local sources. He's a known commodity. You know our resources — it's all volunteers. We get students for a few months during the school year, but it's tough to keep real good tabs on a guy for a few months. There's so many nuts in California. More and more each year."

The law center devoted considerable resources to tracking and monitoring hate groups across the United States. It compiled data on recent activities, recruitment drives, planned rallies, and publications. Despite the region's liberal reputation, hate groups operated aggressively in Northern California.

"I know you are doing what you can." Ray struggled to mute the frustration in his voice.

One of the rock-tossing guys banged a boulder off the dock and into a sea lion. The animal let out a roar. The guy put his hand to his mouth, muffling laughter.

"Is SFPD being helpful?"

"Sort of. They're not about to let this case drop to cold case status at the back of some file cabinet," said Kevin. "It's still high profile. We re-interviewed every resident on the street, but no one remembered seeing a package delivered."

Ray took a sip of coffee and watched as another rock went sailing into the sea lions. Someone yelled at the guy; he gestured and swore back.

"What about the elderly Chinese woman, Mrs. Chin?"

"She still recalls seeing a young white guy with dark hair walking or running up Telegraph Hill just before the explosion. She never saw a face or noted his clothing. She says he disappeared around the corner of an apartment building near Greenwich and Powell streets. We showed her pictures of Cherry, but she couldn't ID him."

The sparse description was more maddening than helpful. But Ray hung a lifetime of hope on the Chinese woman's brief, useless recollection. He pictured the event in his mind, watched the fleeing figure, trying to formulate a face. For Ray, the definitive piece of evidence was not something he needed. As his rage cooled, he knew that the case against the Aryan Knights would rest on Bobby Cherry's shoulders. The case would come together bit by bit, piece by piece, until the sheer mass of the thing, its hot black heart, burst its shell and illuminated the face of the bomber.

"How did the research down South go?" he asked.

"Good. Did some interviews in Alabama. Cherry had a home life that coud only be called a toxic mess. Alcoholic parents and rumors of sexual abuse. There was some sort of family court involvement early on involving a sister. Records were sealed. The sister was removed from the house. Father was charged with rape but the case never went to trial.

"Some of the neighbors we talked to said that Bobby was a nasty little motherfucker as a kid. Lots of fighting, tossed out of school repeatedly, that sort of thing. He also had a habit of torturing animals. No cat was safe from Bobby. He was an active Aryan Knights soldier from his early twenties. He had no prospects there, so he drove his light blue pickup truck to live with a friend in California. That's pretty much the last anyone there has heard of him," said Kevin.

"The boy's chemistry sounds flawed."

"Ray, I know you think this guy is involved. If we learn anything else, you're the first to get a call."

"I know that. I just want to stay on him."

"I know this has special meaning to you." said Kevin.

Ray paused for a moment. "I am taking up some of the work while I am here. Time permitting."

"Of course," said Kevin, looking at his friend.

Kevin leaned over and pulled out a folder. "I put this together for you. All of our work over the past few years." He handed the file to Ray.

"Thanks." Ray opened to the one-inch thick stack of documents neatly clasped inside. He examined the photographs that one of the Law Center investigators had taken during a surveillance last year. Cherry was short and stooped, as if he was constantly warding off a blow from an unseen hand. His black eyes and short dark hair set off noticeably from his pale skin, giving him an intense, almost evangelical look. Ray focused on the eyes. They were phenomenal; they loomed from Cherry's head like separate beings, bulging with unseen pressures. Ray let the image of Cherry's face, his eyes, seep into his brain.

They talked for a while and finished their coffees.

"Let me know if you need anything," said Kevin. "Office space, whatever."

Ray shook his hand and they said good-bye. He felt tense. He walked toward Fisherman's Wharf, where he had parked the car. He stopped to use a public restroom. Inside he saw one of the men who had pelted the sea lions with rocks. The guy tottered a bit on his way to a urinal. He wore a Steelers jacket and baseball cap with the number 0. Without looking at him, Ray went to the sink to wash up. He could smell rock-gut vodka fumes wafting from the guy.

The drunk looked over at Ray. "Hey bro. This a great city or what?"

"Sure is. So why were you tossing rocks at the wildlife?"

The guy paused and then laughed. "Fuck 'em. Why do

you care about some stupid animal like that? That a western thing?"

"No, it's just a human thing. Probably too much for a shitbag like you to comprehend."

The big guy got real quiet. "Well, what you gonna do about it, friend?" he slurred.

Ray ignored him. Always a massive breach of etiquette to speak to another guy in the mens room. Nothing ever came of it. He knew better.

"Hey man, I'm talking to you."

Ray looked at the guy. He was in no hurry. He felt a barely controlled rage flowing through his body. Cherry, the sea lions—all of it hot sap powering his muscles. Some wrath down in his bones needed to be worked off. But there was no need to start anything. The guy was just drunk.

"Fuckin' A, buddy—"the drunk reached out and grabbed Ray's shirt. The guy was big and strong but Ray could see his belly flopped over his belt. The guy had another characteristic often paired with physical heft: he was very slow. Ray slipped the guy's grasp. Then he pivoted on his left foot as he had been trained, as he had done ten thousand times before, swinging his right leg and turning it into a scythe. The knobby bone of his instep thudded into the meat of the guy's thigh. The guy went down like he'd been poleaxed. He cried out in pain and writhed on the tile.

Standing over him, Ray still felt irritated. He unzipped his fly and pissed all over the guy, soaked his chest and head. The guy stared at him with a look of befuddled pain.

"Jesus, my fucking leg!" The drunk held his quadriceps, moaning. He looked damp. "You fuckin' pissed on me!" His voice was high. "What the hell!"

Ray zipped up and adjusted his pants. "Just marking my turf. It's a western thing." Then he left the guy on the bathroom floor and walked outside.

Chapter 26

R ay walked his anger off with a long slow stroll to the house on Telegraph Hill. He took a seat in the kitchen and read the newspaper. The front page was devoted to another anthrax scare. A packet with white powder and a threatening note was sent to a clinic in Brookline, Massachusetts. The white powder had turned out to be flour. The sender handled the envelope so many times that fingerprints were lifted and matched to an out-of work pharmaceutical salesman on Cape Cod. For every criminal mastermind, there were ten cretins: the cruel algebra of intelligence applied across the masses.

He thought again of the carnage in Marin and called Hulme for an update. After the shooting, the Asians had cleaned up quickly. There were no bodies left for the cops to tag. But the Ashtanga staff was terrified. The police were still hot for him to call. Ray promised to get back to them.

The Asians were smart: no bodies, no evidence. But on that hill, he had run over one man and shot another at close range. Although he couldn't be sure, the possibility of both men surviving was slim. But it felt easier to deal with anonymous bodies. He hoped he never learned the names of those two men.

Ray spent over an hour on the phone with a cop from Marin. They wanted to interview him and Tania in person at the station. He told them they were in hiding, and Tania was unsure about making a statement. The cop, a young guy, was not happy with that decision. Ray told him that they were the victims but didn't want to press charges. The cop yelled a bit and Ray ended the call. He got up, knocked gently on Tania's door. She told him to come in, and she sat up abruptly.

"How are you feeling?" he asked

"OK." She rubbed her eyes. "What do we do now?"

"Police want you to come in for an interview."

"No way."

"That's what I said."

"They can't protect me."

"Probably not. But neither can I. You should think it over."

She said nothing. He sat down on the thick cotton blanket covering the bed.

"I talked to Lucas, the attorney. He wants to meet, if you're agreeable. I didn't set a time yet."

Ray walked into the kitchen while Tania got ready. They were starving. Antonio came back with some Thai food: shrimp with a chili sauce and chicken with yellow curry. "I'm warning you," he said, "I like my food spicy. It clears your head." They ate and drank while Ray filled in Antonio on the day's events. He watched Tania for signs of stress, but she seemed rejuvenated. As did he. Ray decided that they would to stay at Antonio's that night. No need to be on the streets.

Something was nagging him about Lucas. He decided that he would review a certain item, a small matter, the next morning. He had long ago learned that intuition was a king who did not tolerate disobedience.

Later that night, he lay in bed in the front bedroom. He dozed off listening to faint strains of an electric guitar coming from the Saloon. He dreamt of his old home, the basketball court and the glittering green grass in the fenced yard. A gurgling sound. The yard flooded with a milky-blue liquid. Something moved beneath the turgid azure, a bubbling. A fin slit the surface. He slipped beneath the ghostly murk, struggling to find his footing. The black fin jerked toward him as he slipped up to his neck, deeper and deeper into the wetness. Above the fence, a leering face appeared, a man watching. He could not make it out. Then some unseen thing hammered his legs.

He woke and got out of bed. Red digits on the clock read 7:21 AM. He went to the bathroom and took a long hot shower. Then he put on a pair of jeans, a blue shirt, and combed his hair. He left a note on the table and headed out to the cool dawn.

Pelicans dove through the cold waters of the San Francisco Bay. The scentless salt air of the bay gusted over the hills. He walked down Telegraph Hill, headed up Powell, and right on Jackson. He turned left onto Polk Street. He passed two cafes that battled for customers by perching enormous cinnamon rolls in the window. He evaluated the offerings of both cafes, entered the cleaner of the two. He bought a cinnamon roll, and sat down in a seat by the window. Watching shards of glaze fall to his plate. The sugar kick-started him. Two fine young things entered the cafe, fresh from an all-night club, platform shoes, toes exposed, midriff bare. Hooker chic. After fifteen minutes, he headed south on Polk Street to the library.

The most frequent visitors to the library stood waiting by the enormous doors: college students facing semester-breaking possibilities, a couple of seventy-year old bibliophiles, a homeless man waiting to warm up in the magazine section. Ray was a little envious of the homeless guy's grubby lassitude — he could spend hours reading peacefully. Ray took his place in line. The wooden Italianate doors rumbled open and a small waifish woman stepped out over the threshold. She gave a halfhearted good morning.

Ray secured a spot at a terminal, and surfed to the home page of the Massachusetts Board of Bar Overseers. In the search section he entered "Michaels, Lucas" and the results came back: Lucas B. Michaels, member since 1958. Law School: U.C. Berkeley. Undergraduate: Boston College.

He then walked over to the reference section, where the scent of rarely opened books permeated the air. He looked through several lawyer guides, but most volumes only went back to the 1980s. Older volumes were on microfiche.

After reviewing several pages of microfiche, he found the listing for San Francisco circa 1958: Lucas had been employed at the Law Office of Richard Scheckman, 86 Sansome Street, San Francisco. The note indicated that the firm's practice was limited to criminal defense.

He checked an index of news articles from 1957 to 1965 — there were 44 sheets in all. After an hour, he looked at a black and white photo with an article about Lucas Michaels, young attorney about town. The date was August 14, 1961. The headline: *Police Arrest One in Chinatown Gun Battle*. A photo showed a young man with chiseled cheekbones and short, black hair that stood straight up as if he were being jolted with major voltage.

The article described how during the early morning hours, police officers had responded to an emergency call: four Chinese men had exchanged gunfire at the intersection of Stockton and Pacific. When police arrived, they chased a man who was bleeding from gunshot wounds. He was later identified as Ralph Ho Chen. The police suspected that the incident was the latest in a series of battles between Chinatown tongs.

Ray followed the story as it had developed. The district attorney returned with an indictment against Ralph Ho Chen, a reputed member of the notorious Black Fist Triad, for his role in the 1957 execution of two Chinatown merchants in the basement of the Blue Moon Restaurant on Vallejo Street.

Mr. Chen's attorney was identified as Lucas Michaels, an attorney with the criminal defense firm Sheckman & Riley. Lucas had issued a statement on behalf of his client: "These charges are baseless, false, and without merit. My client will be exonerated once all facets of the incident are evaluated by a jury of intelligent and reasonable people."

"Well spoken, counsel," Ray said to himself softly.

Lucas had porked him nicely, Ray thought. The lost little girl routine. He looked at his watch and then hurried from the library.

Chapter 27

R ay walked back to Antonio's house on Kearny Street. The streets were busy now: last night's drunks hunting for a morning omelet; elderly Chinese women collecting cans from trash barrels; skinny joggers blowing out their knees on the steep hillsides. The scent of grilled chicken and lemon at Il Pollaio almost derailed him on Columbus, but he soldiered on.

He entered the house, and saw Tania sitting on a leather sofa. He stared for a moment at her body. She had a natural grace that was evident even in repose. She was curled comfortably into the fabric, her cinnamon skin lighter against the dark leather chair. She was reading a book about old Hollywood westerns, one of Antonio's consuming passions.

"How are you? You look rested."

"Yes, I needed to sleep. Where were you?"

"Finishing up some research. On the client." He sighed. "Which is often the most important work you do." Tania put her book down. Ray went to the kitchen, got a glass of water, and returned to the living room. "I spoke with Lucas last night. I thought I knew him — at least I knew of his reputation in Boston. But I found out this morning that Lucas worked as a criminal defense lawyer in San Francisco during the 1950s and 1960s. One of his clients was a Black Fist member named Ralph Chen."

"I know him. "Tania said.

"How?"

"Well, I know of him. He's now a boss of the snakeheads. He started the Mexican pipeline, running Chinese immigrants into the U.S. from Mexico. That's how a lot of girls made it into the U.S. Take a boat to Mexico, and then walk across the border."

"How do you know this?'

"He knew many of the girls. He lives in the East Bay. Lots of girls have been to his place. He's pale and fat for a Chinese man. Like a big scallop. He talks about his work all the time."

Ray said, "Well, I don't think it's just a coincidence that Lucas represented Chen, and now he just happens to be looking for you. You don't just stop representing these guys. Once you're accepted into the inner circle, you tend to get involved for the long haul. Whether you want to or not."

Tania sighed. "Well, what do we do now? First you appear, then Moon, and then I almost get killed by those guys yesterday. And now you're saying this lawyer probably hired the guys who tried to kill me? My life's coming apart since you came here. I know you didn't—"

"Tania, you lived like a caged animal," he said. "How long were you going to hide out with the new age fraud at Ashtanga?"

"She's not a fraud."

"No, I liked her actually. But you weren't safe there for long. I found you easily. After just a few days of work." He paused. "I need to think about this meeting with Lucas." Ray walked out of the room.

* * *

Tania walked back inside her room. She checked the hallway and shut the door. Then she slumped into a cushioned chair, put her head back. She was frustrated with Ray. Who the hell was he, turning her hideout into a battle zone? If she had not been completely happy, then at least she was working to get there.

Still, she admired what he had done. And she had to admit: he was partly right. How long was she going to work in the yoga center kitchen, baking breads for the yoga enthusiasts, keeping out of the light like a cockroach? She was just existing up there. Except for a few brief early morning trips, she realized she had not left the center grounds for over ten days.

In her heart, she knew that her time in Marin was not going to last long.

She felt exposed. But Ray's interference also made her feel furious and alive. She peered out at the Golden Gate Bridge, fog billowing beneath the bridge supports. She understood now that she was a darting obsession to them, someone worth thinking about. Someone worth killing. Her time running had not changed anything. She had misjudged her importance to them. All those men, after all, had been at Ashtanga yesterday morning for the sole purpose of executing her. And she escaped because of a stranger's intervention. She pictured again the men she had seen killed. The green silence of the hills fractured by gunshots. The bump as the tires rolled over the body. She wondered again about Moon, about the other people at the yoga center.

She had run. But they had found her again. She tried to plan and her thoughts were borne back to her old life. The painful memory returned, that day when she left. A country removed, one full of color, deep red, somber, her old home in Hong Kong, the windows looking over the bay. A young girl basking in the adoration of a loving father. Her father had been a businessman, head of a computer hardware wholesaler that sold cheap Korean-made hard drives to overseas dealers. He had grown up bone-poor in Shanghai—"the city of true Chinese" he told her—and he kept the friendships of his youth, installing many of his friends in high positions. He lived hard, allowing a seamy side of the business to flourish along with legitimate ventures, gray-market and counterfeit goods that were funneled through various companies by his friends, all of them longtime triad members. Tania's mother, his first love, became ill and died shortly after Tania was born. He later married for a second time, a Hong Kong beauty, Victoria Chang, a marriage that her politically connected family received coolly. Tania had never been close with her father's second wife. She thought the two of them showed little emotional love, but there was something that drew them together. She could never figure it out, some hard, flinty agreement she could never decipher. He spent little time with his second wife Victoria, who spent most of her time in the U.S., but he lavished attention on Tania. In return, she gave him the gift of her youthful exuberance, and her pride at being his daughter.

Her father's sudden death dropped a black shroud on her happiness. For a year, she grieved. She noticed little of events around her, the cold paper hustle of moving a dead man's earthly belongings through the courts. Victoria Chang was appointed executrix of his estate. She was efficient, uncompromising. Never talkative about her family or origins, she controlled her husband's finances and began to invest those funds in Hong Kong businesses, most notably a series of subsidiaries of a company called the Pan-Pacific Trading Company. Victoria told Tania that the family investments in Pan-Pacific were safe: they were handled by relatives who were experienced businessmen.

In the months after her father's death, various businessmen arrived to meet with Victoria and her assistants. One evening, Tania was instructed to meet Victoria in the study, her favorite room in the house. Her father had assembled a wonderful collection of books on architecture, poetry, literature, and history. Burgundy walls, oak paneling, the scent of old paper—a room of dusty comforts.

Victoria sat behind the desk. A small lamp shone a yellow cone on the brown wood. Victoria fingered a large white envelope and wore an aggrieved look on her face.

Sitting to one side were two Chinese men Tania had seen on several occasions. One man had a dark, narrow face tapered like an ax, with long, fine hands. His long frame covered in an expensive wool suit. The other, thick and flush with years of hard drinking, was dressed in a gray herringbone jacket which emphasized his belly fat. He scanned papers from his briefcase.

Victoria made introductions. "Mr. Chu, this is my

daughter." The tall man nodded, bowed slightly. "Mr. Deng." The fat man barely acknowledged her.

"As you know, I am the executrix for your father's estate. With some assistance, we have completed the review of legal issues relating to the estate distribution. I had hoped the news would be better. But the estate faces serious problems."

Victoria leaned toward at Tania. "Your father has left us in difficult circumstances, Tania. Although this may come as a surprise to you, your father was a gambler. And he has left us with considerable debts."

Tania shifted to interrupt, but Victoria raised her hand.

"Please allow me a moment to explain. We have debts, Tania, debts that your father's estate must meet. Debts to people who do not expect to be kept waiting. There is no other way. Gambling is a disease. A disease that hurts many people, many families. We cannot claim that we are being treated unfairly. As is customary, both the assets and debts of the deceased pass through the estate to the heirs. In this case, we inherit only debts. The debts of your father. And my husband."

Tania felt her stomach knot and her breath tighten. "I cannot believe that my father owes money to anyone." The men threw her a lazy glance.

"The debts are real," replied Victoria. "Now we are called to answer for those debts. With my advisors—she gestured to the two men—we outlined a plan whereby the assets, about $37.2 million worth of real property and stock, will pass to a Hong Kong-based investment corporation. And in time, with wise management, the debts will be paid out of the managed money. We will also realize income after the debts are paid."

"Do we have some proof of these debts?" asked Tania. She had never seen any sign that her father gambled. "It's not like him."

"Gamblers don't get receipts, Tania," said Victoria.

"Then I don't believe it."

The tall man Victoria had called Mr. Chu moved to the wall

where a Japanese katana sword hung. The blade shimmered below a wood handle wrapped in cord. The sword had been presented to Tania's father by one his oldest friends.

Victoria stood up. "I also demanded that an audit take place. I'm not sure we have much choice at this point. We need to process the sale of several properties immediately."

The tall man lifted the sword from its hanger, and walked across the room. The steely sharpness glittered in the faint light. He studied the weapon, intensely interested in the blade. He tested the edge with a fingertip.

Tania felt a warmth breath over her shoulder, a sudden heaviness as the other man, Deng, leaned forward, pressing her down with his bulk. She cried out. Hands gripped her right hand, pulled it out. Pressed it forcefully to the table, splayed the fingers out. She was gasping for breath, but any movement was impossible.

She heard Victoria's voice. "I don't think that is necessary," she said. "Tania, we need to sign certain documents today and these problems will pass. These are harsh people. We can all move on." Tania wondered at Victoria's calmness.

Mr. Deng continued to push his bulk into her. The lights were dim and she smelled sweat and stale food on the chunky man's breath. In front of her, Mr. Chu tapped the table lightly with the sword, swirled it as if he were writing with a giant pen.

"The estate is not sufficient to cover the money your father owed. We have to transfer the funds today. Tania, you are young. An agency run by the creditors in San Francisco will assist you in finding work. You leave tomorrow. They have arranged a plane. They ask that no inquiries be made about the finances. We have no other options, Tania."

Her back was hurting. She scrambled for a way to defy the crude demands of these men. She would talk to someone, there were people, lawyers her father had known, who could help.

Victoria added, "If we can resolve this today, they have

told me that your sister will be left out of this problem."

Something reptilian and cold shot through her gut. Victoria opened the envelope that had been lying on her desk, dumping the contents on the desk in front Tania. Plane tickets and an itinerary. Cash in rubber bands, as well as a notebook. There were also several photographs. Victoria slid the photographs towards Tania, fanning them out like a deck of playing cards.

"I saw these just one hour ago. They told me these were taken yesterday in Shanghai."

Tania picked up a photo and saw her half-sister, Lin. They looked like recent photos. Lin held two plastic bags of groceries as she walked down Siping Road in the Hongkou District, probably after shopping for fresh shrimp at a small market she loved. Lin had called her that night, and spoke about the dinner she was cooking. The next photo showed the faded sign of the movie theater next to the apartment where she lived. A third photo showed Lin wearing a red hat, sitting at a café and sipping tea on a leisurely afternoon.

In each photo, her sister was clearly oblivious of the photographer. No shadow of concern darkened her face. She was blind to the watcher, just living. Tania craned her neck and looked at each photo again. Lin's fragile life, no longer secure in the anonymous city, but pinned and squirming in front of Tania like a butterfly in an entomological display. Both she and her sister without family or means. Both vulnerable to the specter of sudden violence.

The tall man moved to Tania, the sword gripped with offhanded elegance. He spoke in a low voice. "None of this is your fault. Honor your father's memory. Honor your ancestors." He named casinos where her father had bankrupted himself, businesses that were owed funds, restaurants and nightclubs where he had run exorbitant tabs. Victoria sat impassively at the desk, while they beat Tania down with misdirection and innuendo. "Let's take care of this today, forever," the tall man said. "And then you start on the path to a new tranquility."

Tania listened to the words, unbelieving, the edge of her focus worn away. Her mouth was dry. Her wrists hurt. She felt terribly alone then, and a black mood descended. Her sister at the café, oblivious. A deep sob erupted from inside, the shame of it, all this in her own father's house. A daughter's love for her father, purest on earth.

"Honor your father," the fat man repeated. His sickly-sweet odor, the waxy light behind the desk. Victoria sat in the shadows, her hands illuminated.

There was no one here for her, Tania realized. Then she took the pen in stiff fingers and signed the documents, transferring the property out of her possession forever.

Chapter 28

Afternoon arrived in a gray curtain. Ray slumped on the couch and brooded over Lucas's deception. He was rotting here, he felt it, the inactivity heavy as sludge in his veins. The horror of almost delivering Tania to her pursuers. Like the lethal package that had once been delivered to his old home, when he wasn't there, and someone else was. The thin line between a brilliant performance and ripping your lungs out at a funeral.

Lucas would be arriving soon. He got up and flicked on the computer, entered his password. He looked at his contact information for Lucas, and typed a message into his phone: Pantera Cafe, Romolo Place, North Beach. See you @ 4:00 PM.

A touch of venom in his brain, he hit send.

Ray made himself a cup of coffee. Rainwater rushed in torrents down the gutter. Tania was sleeping. She was still angry, and had not spoken to him after learning of Lucas's deception. Ray accepted her coldness. She was bending under the strain.

Ray telephoned Dominique, and updated her on his suspicions about Lucas. "I may ask you to go to your news sources with this later. The usual bullshit: 'Prominent Attorney Plotted Murder; 40 years as a gangster's bag man.' Some bullshit the good citizens can chew on over a bagel."

"We have to consider the possibility that he'll sue for libel. Are you certain that's the full story? Is there a chance he can explain? All you have is this old news story."

"Oh, I'm sure he'll have some explanation," said Ray. "I just want to be there to see if he stains his underpants with the effort. Lawyers don't like being questioned. But I think he'll have to explain himself with more than just coincidence theory."

"OK. I'll think about where to place it," said Dominique.

"Just to play this a bit further, let's draft an affidavit. He'll never sign it but we'll play the game. "

"He'll be insulted," she said. "His Burberry tie will start smoking."

"Maybe there's a way we can link him to sex with underage boys."

"No one will blink," she said. "Underage horses might cause him problems. PETA is active in California."

"Go with it."

Ray showered. He put the Beretta semiautomatic in the shoulder holster, strapped it on, then dressed in a blue pinstriped, double-breasted suit with a lavender shirt and tie. A bit bulky; he'd leave the coat unbuttoned. He killed an hour reading a book from Antonio's eclectic library: a biography of a Russian mage named Gurdjeiff, who reportedly had developed telekinesis and could hurl himself off a thirty-foot stage without suffering injuries. Ray found the book oddly reassuring: its quirky mysticism transcended the nasty business at hand.

At 3:30 he left the house. He walked to Union Street and headed down the slope of Telegraph Hill to North Beach, just another businessman transacting the dealings of the day.

On Powell Street, he gazed down toward his old apartment. Chaos in the street that day, panicked neighbors. The sun was blazing; the sun always seemed to be out for the big disasters in California. Sifting for evidence. He could never forget the human sleet scattered all over the place. Each night he dreamt it again, walking through the house. Then the explosion, the burning, and the voice of the friendly cop trying to stop him from seeing: "Nothing to see in there, sir." Then her voice, soft and murmurous as water in a dying creek. She was telling him something. The tea bags, they were out of tea bags again.

That day gouged his overheated mind over and over and over, etching a ravine through his brain. He just wanted to stop the fire.

Ray shook his head and walked the gentle rise of Columbus

Avenue toward downtown. The Transamerica pyramid rose majestically in front of him, seemingly floating on the tip of Columbus, dominating the view. He walked past the Steps of Rome, the restaurant quiet as young bloods sipped espressos and checked soccer scores from the Italian leagues. At Columbus and Grant trucks were double-parked while workers unloaded pink carcasses of freshly killed pigs from the steel beds.

He took a left on Broadway. Strip joints lined the streets, red doors heavily locked, painted with quaint come-ons from the 1960's — *Groovy Girls in Female Love Duo*. A neon nipple flashed blue while hawkers corralled tourists into paying ten bucks for pisswater beer.

He took a sharp left past the strip joints into Romolo Place. He stopped, looking back into Broadway. Traffic roared by, and people walked and shopped. Nothing unusual.

Looking up, he saw the sign for the Pantera Cafe, emblazoned with the silhouette of a running panther. He took a deep breath, pictured in his mind the strands of the last few days coalescing into a black web. He just hoped he wasn't the one about to fly into the center. Then he walked into the Pantera.

A long wooden bar flanked by carved wooden lion heads; a clock no longer functioning, with gold arms fixed at 12:03. A series of tables and chairs, red in color, arranged in a dining area. A jukebox played opera music — Puccini, Verdi, and other classics, leavened with a sonic dose of Frank Sinatra. A few solitary souls at the bar: several older men, a few creative arts types in meditative postures over their drinks, and one young woman talking quietly on a cell phone.

At a table near the rear wall, Lucas Michaels sat in silver-haired grace, debonair in a dark suit and red patterned tie. He sipped a cocktail. Ray looked briefly at two Asian men sitting at a table to the left. Late thirties, well-dressed, they were drinking and talking casually. Too casually, in Ray's mind: a wolfishness still hung off them. And the drinks were clear, probably water. Real warriors needed no lubrication. The men glanced over at Ray. One of them, shorter and leaner than his associate, stood and walked to the restroom. His bearing showed a fighter's flexibility. Ray would have to deal with him first, if anything came of it.

Lucas looked up and smiled a Sunday afternoon smile. "Hello Ray."

"Hi Lucas."

Ray sat down. An efficient dark-haired waitress commandeered the floor, and Ray ordered a gin and tonic.

"Well, it's good to see you Ray. Your work was outstanding."

"Thanks. Good to see you."

Lucas looked around. "Where is she?"

"Tania made a decision to delay the meeting."

Lucas eyes went flat and tight for a second before flooding back to a cool sheen. "Why? Is she OK?"

"Tania is singing a song of self-preservation, Lucas. One that will pull her into a new life."

Lucas gave him a quizzical look.

"She told me this morning that she wasn't ready to meet yet."

"Where is she?" Lucas said calmly.

"She needs to clarify some outstanding issues."

Lucas said nothing. He looked irritated, and shuffled his glass on the table. He didn't like this ridiculous riddling at all. "I am paying you well, you were to find her, and I thought we had agreed that she would be here."

"Yes, I know. But things are evolving even as we speak. Tania is in danger, Lucas. She's hiding from an Asian gang called the Black Fist." Ray paused and watched as Lucas's eyes widened a fraction. "Ever hear of them?"

"No," said Lucas softly.

"I thought you might recall the name. You represented one of them, Ralph Chen, early in your career. And then represented several more gang members over the years.

She is concerned about that connection. I'm sure you can understand."

Lucas swayed slightly, a cobra evaluating its strike zone.

"That representation occurred many years ago, and was the start of my career as a defense attorney," said Lucas. "It is not relevant to anything happening now."

"I understand. But this connection is causing Tania a lot of concern."

"Not important," snapped Lucas. He took a drink, then jammed the glass to the table.

"Wrong. Very important. If I have some reason to question the purpose of an investigation, then I might ask for assurances. In this case, I have reason to ask."

"I did not hire you to look into my background," Lucas said thickly.

"Your background is only part of the story," said Ray. "When we spoke by telephone after our little run-in in Marin, you had an interesting take on what had happened. Was there another bird whispering in your ear?"

Lucas's face flushed slightly. "You are being well-paid to handle this matter, and I expect you to produce the—her, Tania."

"The story is too sweet," said Ray. "Very good though, Lucas, appealing to my nobler instincts. How were you going to do it? Right in front of me, after I brought her to you? I can only assume you hadn't thought that out either. Because maybe you're nothing more than a bag man, despite the law school education."

Lucas stared. A smugness flattened his face, and his hand pecked at his glass on the table. He laughed abruptly as if the matter were too petty to consider. "This is ridiculous!"

Ray could see his mind working, rolling the jagged facts into a comfortable arrangement. Men like Lucas did not admit anything. They were beyond reach, glossy creatures that existed in another dimension. Lucas specialized in warping words to his benefit. A lifetime devoted to studying ways to confuse, delay, muddy up the trail. He was the subject of news articles, he lived in a big city, made sure his yearly income was in the upper echelon. He was a middle-aged white lawyer, and that still counted for something. Lucas gathered himself up.

"You are an old-fashioned hero, Ray. You really are. What a fool. I think you've fallen in love with her. I'll press every advantage I have professionally to see that your actions are well known among the bar. You'll be ruined."

"Please Lucas. I know as many lawyers in Boston as you do. Probably more. But we need to discuss some of this stuff on record." Ray pulled out a tape recorder. "California doesn't permit one-party taping, so I need you to OK it. . ."

"What's this!" Lucas looked askance at the recorder. "Are you joking? Put that fucking thing away." His brow looked sweaty. "Assuming that there are certain considerations that limited what I could tell you, your theory is not based in reality. Tania is the blood relative of my client. I already told you this. If they became involved. . .. "

Ray let him talk, and watched his face, making slow circles from the eyes, eyelids, and brow, down to the mouth and then back. Lucas's mouth was drawn into a tight box, harsh and ragged. Clearly, he was angry about Tania's absence. But there was something else. His fingers tugged at his collar, and he returned to his constant theme: "I need to see Tania today. Now."

"She won't be here today, Lucas. Not a chance."

"Where is she — "

"Just tell me what's happening," said Ray, smoothing the air above the table with his hand. "How long have you represented Victoria Chang?"

At the mention of Victoria, Lucas' face twitched with subterranean irritation.

"Do you need to scratch?" asked Ray.

"What?"

"What does she have on you? Why the mystery?"

Lucas shifted in his seat, trying to position himself comfortably. "In 1958, I was a young lawyer with a top criminal defense firm here in San Francisco. One of my early clients was Ralph Chen. He was a low-level soldier for a Chinese gang, involved with minor street violence against other gangs in Chinatown. He was indigent. There is nothing more to the story. I performed a legal service and my relationship with that client ended. It's unfair to judge a defense attorney on who he represented years ago. These are people who get churned up by the justice system without any representation. You know that. I agreed to represent him, and I am proud of the legal work I did on his behalf. Now I am ending this conversation and bid you good day. You are no longer authorized to continue working."

Ray raised his hand, placed his palm against Lucas's chest. A stirring from behind the table. The two Asian men dropped their feigned indifference and layered their attention toward the table. Ray kept his voice low.

"Lucas, you earn a living through words. And like a lot of attorneys, you figure as long as you're running your mouth, you must be making money. But you should consider how your famous voice has played so far. Quite a few dissonant chords, Lucas. The Marin hit was botched, and I'm guessing that someone will be very unhappy to hear of another failure. You won't get to Tania through me. Not today, not ever. Her testimony is being memorialized. You made a foray into the street business of your clients, but that's not an easy thing to pull off. Will you consider an alternative?"

Lucas paused. His voice started, then wavered and went out, extinguished by a chill from some desperate corner of his life. Ray realized that Lucas was terrified.

Then Lucas sneered. "You think it's all wrapped up so tightly? Go ahead with your little fucking news story!" Lucas jabbed his finger at Ray. "I represented a gangster in the 1960's. So what? That's the way it is, Ray! We defend clients with dirty pasts."

"But now you're dirty, Lucas. That's the difference."

"Your case is built around a hooker, Ray. No one believes hookers."

"She was in the trade," said Ray. "But you're the real whore."

Ray sat back in his chair. "Come to Jesus, Lucas. Before your master.."

"I'm through with this conversation!" Lucas hissed.

Ripples of heat and animosity emanated from the small table as Ray stood up. People were turning towards them now. The two Asian men looked at Ray with undisguised hunger, awaiting some sign from Lucas.

But the sign never came. Lucas sat at the table, shaking with rage and something else; the two men stood still, bad intentions frozen in anticipation. A fine-looking Latina abruptly walked past the table towards the door; she had curly black hair and a slender body perched on open-toed sandals. She looked at Ray with concern in her eyes, sensing the hostility of the meeting. Ray followed her out the door and left the Pantera. After he walked down Romolo Place and reached Broadway, his body flooded with relief that he wasn't being blasted with anything other than Northern California sunshine.

Chapter 29

R ay felt certain that the bar was being watched. He looked around. People walked the sidewalks, peering into cafes and restaurants. A homeless guy with a brown beard rolled around on the sidewalk in front of a corner liquor store.

Ray headed north on Grant Street past the blues bars. He took a quick right, crossed Green Street and then walked into Genoa Place. The backs of three-story apartments loomed over the narrow alleyway. For a second he regretted entering—the alley was too isolated. He picked up his pace, jogging to the end of the cool, deserted alley, peering cautiously onto Union Street. No one stood watching, no male-packed cars menacing a corner.

So this was the end of the line for Lucas. Ray had seen rich clients—politicians, executives, celebrities—reduced to frantic phone calls when the props failed, and the arc of their burnished life thudded into the ground. The right neighborhood was a trap, and a career could be pissed away on one astoundingly dumb decision. He had no idea why Lucas was working for the Triad, but clearly, he was deeply involved.

Ray looked back. A blue Acura blocked the alley entrance. A tinted window simmered and slid silently down.

Ray sprang out of sight behind the corner of the building. He ran up Union Street and saw a cab stop at the intersection and begin to accelerate. He yelled, and the cab's brake lights flashed red. He ran to the cab, opened the left car door and jumped inside. "Go right on Kearny. Then down Vallejo to Sansome." The driver gunned the musty Chevrolet up the hill. Turned right, then left on Vallejo. Ray pulled out the nine millimeter, keeping it low. The driver turned left on Sansome, the sheer face of Telegraph Hill rising high overhead on their left. They headed toward Fisherman's Wharf.

Too late.

The blue Acura surged into view on the right. Ray glanced over, caught images— sunglasses, half-rolled windows, taut faces, a gun barrel pointing. The cabby glanced over and hammered the brakes. The front end of the taxi dove earthward. The sour smell of burning rubber. Several popping sounds, and the rock-face of the hill smoked. Ray watched as the Acura tried to stop, its wheels smoking the pavement. The car skidded down the street, trailing a smoky wake. Other cars slowed or veered off to one side.

Ray could hear honking and yelling. A crash as two cars collided behind them. The cabby was wailing wildly, unable to gather himself, his taxi vulnerably becalmed in the middle of Sansome Street.

Ray flung open the door and leaped from the cab, racing toward the base of the hill. A long cement staircase meandered up the steep side of Telegraph Hill. About thirty yards up, the path turned steeply into thick underbrush. A series of wooden steps ran uphill several hundred feet.

Ray ducked behind a cement column. He looked back at the street. No one was following. The blue Acura peeled away. A few cars were tangled in the middle of the street. People stood in the middle of the street, gaping, while others yelled about the gunshots, urban tales of narrow escapes.

A German couple thought they had stumbled upon a film set; they approached several men who looked vaguely famous and asked for autographs.

Sirens in the distance.

Squatting behind the column for a few minutes, Ray scanned the area. He turned and hiked up past small, shaded cottages on either side, accessible by way of narrow paths lined with century plants and pine. Wild parrots flitted and chattered overhead. Every few minutes, Ray looked back warily, but he felt better here. Telegraph Hill was a tree-sheltered labyrinth of one way streets and dead ends, alleys that zigzagged over the overgrown hill. He knew the hills well from having walked them almost every day while living in the neighborhood. He would meander through the hidden paths and get back to North Beach.

He squatted on the hillside path for a few more minutes. Watched the ground far below, and monitored any approach from the top of the hill. Coit Tower, smooth and creamy-gray, pronged the sky above him. Music wafted from cars parked on top of the hill, the ominous storm of Led Zeppelin's "Kashmir". Every now and then, a hiker scrambled over the hillside. Some wore designer boots and sipped the remains of a North Beach coffee, walking slowly, rubbing their calf muscles. Others, prepared and determined, maneuvered skillfully over the rocky hill.

Ray sat down on a rock wall. He was done with Lucas. He should stop all work now, and head back to Logan. There was no paying client.

But he couldn't do that. Not with the way things were. He had unearthed a young woman from her sanctuary — inadequate though it was — and now he owed her. He thought of Diana and his old apartment; they had lived at the base this hill, just a few hundred feet down.

Ray looked out at the bay, the sky shot through with orange-pink clouds. Then he dialed Antonio's home. Tania picked up.

"How did it go?"

"Pretty well. I think Lucas made some type of indirect admission — he tried to kill me. Or someone did."

He heard a sharp intake of breath. "Are you OK?"

He relayed the details of the meeting. "Lucas turned out to be nervous and erratic. I think pressure is building on him; he's botched things pretty badly, first in Marin, and again today. Mistakes bring unwanted interest. He's into things that he is not accustomed to, street-level stuff."

"What did he say?"

"He admitted to representing some low-level Triad guy years ago. Not much more. He brought poorly disguised friends to the meeting, two Asian goons. And Lucas's body language told me everything I suspected." Ray glanced around but no one was watching him.

"What do we do now?"

"I need you to stay out of sight. Just relax with Antonio, OK? I'll be traveling for a few days."

"Where are you going?" Tania asked.

"It's time to bring the war home."

"What do you mean?"

"I'm not sure yet. Pondering it. I'll call later."

They said goodbye. He walked to the top of the hill, looking warily. He hailed a cab. The driver raced down Telegraph Hill until he hit Van Ness, timing it perfectly so that the lights eased to green and the cab glided toward Market Street. Ray appreciated the finesse.

He knew that they had no chance to outrun their problem. They were massively outgunned, and there were any number of young bloods who would try to make a mark by assassinating Tania. And probably him too.

He called Dominique and briefed her on the meeting. "The Triad boss mentioned in that report," he said, "time to pay a little visit."

"What is that going to do?"

"I'm not sure. But everyone hates trash dumped on their lawn. I'm just moving trash to where it gets some attention."

A long pause. "You be careful. Need any help?"

"I can get her address from my databases. She may have taken steps not to be found."

"The boss is a she?"

"Yes. Victoria Chang. She's Tania's stepmother."

Dominique was quiet. Ray looked around again. He wanted to keep moving. "I gotta go. Thanks for everything."

"Thank me in person," she said.

"I'll call you."

Chapter 30

The 747 eased its bulk onto the tarmac in East Boston, following the blue lights to the terminal. After the rustle of weary passengers, Ray exited the plane and headed to the rental car section. He wore a cream colored suit over a burgundy silk shirt with a black and silver tie. He wanted a blend of colors that suggested a creative talent, a radical bravado—it went a good distance with gangsters. And bravado was possibly all he really had.

All day long, his frustration had grown. He was uncertain what he could do for Tania. Lucas had reamed him; he should have picked up something earlier, some subtle tick in his demeanor. Maybe he had been too intent on the other aspects of the trip, a return to the city that was once home to all loved. Distracted by the hunt for Bobby Cherry. He had let his customary thoroughness slide.

The Black Fist would never stop hunting Tania, he realized. In the modern world, people could be found easily, as she had been. Privacy was a quaint concept, something smashed open as easily as dashing an egg on concrete. Hiding out like a renegade would only get her killed. Another tactic was needed.

It was past 9:00 PM when Ray arrived in Harvard Square. He drove on Brattle Street where tony shops gave way to grand homes along brick sidewalks. He stopped in front of 101 Brattle Street, a Second Empire Victorian mansion surrounded by an eight foot tall brick wall. The house had been built for Judge James Wagner in 1826. Stately oak and elm shrouded the front yard. A tower rose from the Mansard roof, which combined with the arched dormers to give the house an appearance of edgy watchfulness.

The sense of watchfulness was not misleading. The

property bristled with modern security features, noticeable to only a trained eye. Security cameras rotated silently every twenty feet; motion detectors and parabolic sound detectors had been installed, all under the control of round-the-clock security personnel located in a refurbished carriage house behind the main house. Three armed guards patrolled the perimeter of the walls; two others kept watch in the house.

In June 1957, the Wagner mansion had been purchased by C. Dalton Scott, a respected Boston lawyer. A series of transactions involving real estate trusts obscured the name of the true owner, Paul F. Chang. He moved into the home that summer. Chang modernized the house, making it secure, as if he were a Ming emperor facing his enemies across a barren plain. Which he was, in a sense: he had been installed as the head of the northeast crime syndicate. Years later, in 1978, the house passed into the hands of his hand-picked successor, his only daughter, Victoria Chang.

Victoria Chang was educated in business and the law, taking degrees at the highest academies in Beijing. She was a striking young woman, inheritor of her mother's luxuriant black hair and her father's angular Mandarin features. But hers was a frosty beauty, and few knew her well. In a culture where females had been traditionally praised for their docility, she stepped forward as a paragon of a new breed. Her father noted her keen talents and favorably compared them to the less stellar ones exhibited by his sons. He believed that cultivating an individual's unique talents—regardless of gender—was a sacred duty, and he quickly elevated Victoria to high positions within the syndicate. She married a longtime business associate of the Chang family, a marriage that cemented centuries-old business dealings between the families. Her husband later died unexpectedly, and she never remarried. At age 37, she was dispatched to Boston, where she oversaw the operations of the Black Fist Triad.

Victoria quickly gained a formidable reputation. In 1978, various Chinatown gangs controlled carefully drawn sections of the city, where they demanded payments from merchants operating within the territory. When City Hall began to implement a massive redevelopment scheme for downtown Boston, gangs near Kneeland Street, one of the main areas slated for redevelopment, grew concerned about their soon-to-be shrunken revenue base. One of those gangs, Triple Dragon, was involved in a turf war with Red Horse, a Chinatown gang never expanded beyond heroin trafficking. Triple Dragon was rudderless after a number of its top leaders were imprisoned. In an attempt to salvage its declining fortunes, the tong was pressing for new opportunities. Its members often secretly traded information with other gangs, and these side deals created conflicting loyalties.

On September 21, 1978, local bosses of Triple Dragon and Red Horse met at the Grand Hyatt Hotel on Tremont Street. Over courses of dim sum, they discussed the various problems facing the gangs. But not everyone was enjoying the lunch. A brawl broke out. Gangsters wielding machetes warred with each other until the marble floors were slick with blood. Eight gangsters were killed, six of them Triple Dragon soldiers.

Revenge killings followed, and a full-out war was imminent. There were shootings during daylight hours in local markets, men opening fire near crowded outdoor markets. Bystanders were hit or, in some cases, killed. The growing number of spectacular shootings began to attract the attention of law enforcement.

The ruling counsel of the major triads met and ordered the cantankerous bosses to put aside their quarrels. Outside interference was the great evil that all the triads guarded against. Also, it gave racist Boston cops an excuse to beat and rob Chinese gangsters under the guise of enforcing the law. The honored code of underground warfare was being flagrantly violated.

But the meetings broke down, and Triple Dragon and Red Horse continued their street war. Within a few days, the ruling counsel agreed to sever the offending extremities.

Late at night on October 6, 1978, at the direction of Victoria Chang, a group of Black Fist soldiers fanned out into Chinatown.

The leader of the Triple Dragon, the stylish Ang Lee, was hunched with his crew, playing cards in a sweaty basement behind the Shanghai Restaurant on Tyler Street. He was down $6,000.00. He jabbed at his kung pao shrimp and swore over his relentless bad luck.

His luck soon worsened. In the dark morning hours, he stepped out of a rear door to the restaurant for a cigarette. He was met by three Triad members. One of the men stepped forward and crushed his skull with a pipe. The men shoved his body into the back of a delivery truck and he was never seen again. It was widely speculated among the bosses that Lee had become well-dressed fish chum.

One day later, the Red Horse boss, Paul "Ghost" Zheng, stumbled into his office. His face was minus his nose; a sign around his neck read "No sniffing," a warning to dogs seeking to piss on new turf. His crew growled about revenge. The following week, as Zheng's wife left a local market, she was struck by a car and killed. The matter was determined to be an accident, although bystanders whispered that the driver appeared to be aiming for someone in the narrow quarters. A few days later, Zheng's brother, a restaurant owner, was found garroted in the basement. The family reported the case as a robbery, although no money had been taken.

And so it went, a numbing campaign of violence, directed at selected family members of the warring bosses. The nerveless efficiency of the campaign bled all defiance from the gangs. In less than a month, the bosses agreed to recognize the old Kneeland Street boundary as fully restored. Bereft of leadership, the remnants of Triple Dragon and Red Horse were absorbed by the Black Fist Triad. The media glare was passing to newer scandals and the gangs were left to prey on their own kind amid the teeming streets of Chinatown.

The campaign marked the beginning of the Black Fist's

decades-long dominance of the Northeast vice trade. With each passing year, the Chang family coiled deeper and deeper into the Boston underworld, moving into counterfeit goods, prostitution and drug trafficking. By the late 1990's, cash was laundered through a variety of legitimate businesses: massage parlors, salons, contractors, small restaurants that handled mostly cash transactions. The melding of drug money with legal business revenue proved impossible for law enforcement to track in any meaningful way.

As the businesses prospered—many now wholly legitimate—Victoria Chang continued to oversee triad operations from her mansion in Cambridge. Her youthful beauty had gracefully subsided, and she looked the part she played: hard, aloof, able to tap into old-world connections with the refined touch of a bygone era. She remained the unchallenged head of a multimillion dollar black world.

Ray looked at the house and patted the snub-nosed .357 revolver under his belt. He quickly thought better of it, and placed it under the seat. The metallic weight of the gun did little to reinforce his confidence: the people here would be sufficiently armed to outshoot him, that he was certain. Tonight's maneuver was all finesse.

He drove his Cadillac to the black iron gate barring entry to 101 Brattle Street. A black intercom, almost unnoticeable, was set among the small pines lining the driveway. Ray reached out and rang.

A metallic voice: "Who is calling please?"

"Ray Infantino. I'm here to see Victoria Chang."

"Do you have an appointment, sir?"

"Please tell her I am here on short notice to discuss Tania Kong."

Ms. Chang does not see anyone without an appointment."

"I am certain that she will want to discuss the name Tania Kong. Please tell her that I recently concluded my meeting with Mr. Michaels."

Silence and the intercom went dead. A few minutes later,

it came back on. "Please wait by the gate, sir."

Ray sat with the engine idling, and waited in the darkness. Cars rolled by the entrance way, wheels drumming a rhythmic bump as they crossed the brick crosswalks. He listed to the radio and rehearsed the introduction he had prepared. Then he caught himself—who the hell knew what would work once he was in the house? He needed to stay flexible.

He smelled an earthy tang in the air, and savored the scent.

They let him stew for over an hour before the intercom crackled to life. "Mr. Infantino, please come in."

The gate slid aside and Ray drove inside. He headed up a long, semicircular driveway paved with red brick. He passed by dense yews, forsythia, juniper and hemlock.

The main house was lit here and there with ground lights. Ray pulled up to an iron fence and stepped outside the car. On the porch, he could see a pair of bronze doors.

A well-dressed, unsmiling Asian man appearing to be in his fifties stepped outside. Two young Asian men followed; they were carrying machine guns. "Stop here!" one of them said sharply. The men patted Ray down methodically, fingering his pockets and jacket. He raised his chin and let them poke. Satisfied, they stepped back. Ray walked behind the older man, and entered the front hall.

The house was lavishly decorated. The interior doors were heavy oak, fitted with dark brass handles. The deep red walls were lit by artfully arranged lanterns. Antique wooden chairs inlaid with mother of pearl, silk tapestries. From the immediate room to the left—Ray thought it looked like a drawing room or library—came the scent of leather and old paper.

"Please have a seat," the man said. "Ms. Chang will meet with you in a moment." Then he exited.

Ray sat down on a mahogany colored sofa. A red and gold Chinese opera mask stared back. For a second, he wondered if something had moved behind the hollow eyes. Cherrywood bookshelves lined with hardcover books, mostly Asian and Spanish art.

A door clicked opened. An Asian woman walked into the room. Her hair was pulled back in a chignon. Her porcelain skin, although no longer the flawless cream of youth, gave her a look of indeterminate age. She was dressed in a dark colored suit with white pinstripes. The suit went well with her eyes, which were reptilian and unforgiving. Ray looked hard at those eyes, so luminously out of symmetry with the rest of her preserved elegance. There was nothing withheld in Victoria's bearing, no Zen Buddha bullshit; she wielded considerable authority, wielded it openly. Nothing bombastic or insistent, but Ray could sense that she had long ago decided that it fit her style to show that power was at her command. Ray felt an odd jolt of satisfaction. Here was someone whose appearance matched her reputation.

"Mr. Infantino." She did not offer a hand.

"Ms. Chang."

"Would you like some tea?" she asked with a half-dead smile that quickly slipped off her face.

"Yes, thank you." Within moments, an elderly Chinese man entered the room, bearing a teapot on a tray with two cups. He placed the tray on a dark wooden table next to Victoria, and then departed.

"I am taken aback by your manner of approach today." Victoria's voice was controlled and melodious.

"How so?"

"I am not accustomed to visitors just dropping by my home without prior contact. I expect you have an urgent need, however, and I will try to accommodate you. Please, sit here," she said, pointing to a plush chair. Ms. Chang glided toward her chair and sat down, her face highlighted in muted crimson by a Japanese lamp shade. She poured herself a cup of tea.

"I am here to tell you I have located your stepdaughter, Tania Kong, as directed by Lucas Michaels. She updated me on her recent escapades with the Triad."

Victoria shook her head. "Tania and I do not speak," she

said. Her hands were crossed on her lap.

"Did Lucas tell you he retained me?"

She shook her head slowly. "Please explain your purpose here today."

"Lucas hired me to find a young woman for someone he described as a client. That woman is Tania. After I found her, I suddenly found myself the target of an unhealthy bit of attention. Several men tried to kill her. They were sent by my own client — and your lawyer — Lucas Michaels. I know Lucas represented members of your group many years ago."

Victoria blinked several times before lapsing back into a corporate coolness.

"I do not think Lucas made the decision to involve those men," Ray continued. "I think that certain forces in his world simply required that a poorly executed plan at the Senator Hotel be rectified. But his cleanup attempts have failed. Several times. Your lawyer is slipping in his old age. Maybe it's the warm weather. Maybe they didn't teach executions in law school back in the fifties."

Victoria sipped her tea. "And what does this have to do with me?"

"Beside the fact that the girl is your daughter — if not a daughter by blood? A well-connected WASP lawyer is a great asset, I would think, for someone in your position. A lawyer like that has a pleasing scent. But Lucas overreached. Despite his reputation — or because of it — he has made some powerful enemies. He has a reputation as a showboat. Believe me, there are lawyers in the AGs office in Massachusetts who would love to skewer Lucas. I think he's now close to cooked. Maybe even charred a bit."

Ray paused. "And if in picking him, they get a drift of a larger beast below the surface. . . "

Victoria glanced at something above his shoulder. Ray resisted the temptation to turn around.

"Call off the hunt for Tania," he said. "She is not a threat to anyone here, no matter what she did or did not see."

"Mr. Infantino, I know Lucas professionally. He has advised me for many years. Tania left home on her own years ago. You know what she does, I am sure. She is a whore. A liar. Whatever conspiracy theories you have do not interest me. That is where it ends. Your other references are not at all familiar to me."

"I don't think that I misinterpret your influence—if not your involvement—to date, Ms. Chang," Ray said. "Whatever you think of Lucas, he panicked. Our meeting yesterday had an unfortunate, fiery conclusion. Another shootout in San Francisco. Nothing gets the law's attention like a Minnesota tourist getting smoked on the cable car."

Ray shook his head, opened his hands. "I am just beginning to explore the ties between Lucas and your organization. But before we let slip the dogs of war, I wanted to come here. We need to remove one soldier from the battlefield."

Victoria gave no sign of having heard. She sat still, a flat look to her eyes. Ray looked at those delicate hands, thin, long, vampirish. But the public face of that darkness, composed and elegant. He felt chilled in that room, that close to her. He thought of a line from a book he had loved as a child— 'All that is gold does not glitter.' Here he beheld its terrible reverse: splendor veiling the devil's face.

"I will consider your words," Victoria said, "although I am not familiar with much of what you have said. You're not making sense. Now I must call our meeting to a close."

She stood up. "Please leave a card." She gestured to a table where sat a gold tray fashioned in the shape of a maple leaf.

"I look forward to hearing from you." Ray got up slowly, picked up his leather card case and placed a card in the tray. Like handing a map of your home to an assassin, he thought.

Victoria Chang sat back in her chair and receded into the shadows. Ray nodded and walked toward the foyer. He saw no one, but sensed someone peering at him from the darkened recesses. Wordlessly, the older man who had greeted him appeared, and led him to the door.

Ray stepped out into the darkness, feeling his bones loosen a bit. He felt relieved, and a little burst of adrenaline spiked through his veins.

Victoria Chang had been a brutal read. He had no idea how she had digested his offering. He walked to his car and drove down the long driveway. The gate opened and he drove right onto Brattle Street. He rolled down his window. The scent of spring, dirt-rich and pungent. The maple pollen covering the sidewalks with a luminous green dusting. He inhaled deeply.

He drove back on Memorial Drive and headed to his home on the Charles River. He went upstairs and put his head on a cool pillow. He lay there for a long time, meandering down murky corridors of his mind.

* * *

Victoria sat quietly watching the small video screen. Ray Infantino's car drove away from her property. She directed her staff to leave her alone for the next hour. Then she turned to the well-dressed man who had let Ray into the house and then watched the entire meeting through a hidden aperture in the wall.

"Impressions?' she asked.

"The visit was a desperate move," he replied, sitting next to Victoria.

"Perhaps. His unannounced arrival showed a certain boldness that I think should be nipped in the bud," said Victoria. She looked again at the video screen. Ray Infantino was gone. "But I admire the tactic. The simple act of getting in front of me, where I could see him, taste his skin."

"It's a tactic we favor," he said.

"Yes, a solid policy. I think his action needs an appropriate response. A meaningful gesture. But his message has some substance to it."

"Our old associate botched things badly," said the man.

"The years may have strengthened our friendship, but

there are signs that time has eroded his business acumen. We will arrange a resolution," she said. "He's tired. It is time he passed those duties to another lawyer." Victoria sipped her tea.

Then the man walked to another desk, picked up a secure line and dialed California.

Chapter 31

The telephone rang and Ray picked up—the electric voice of the wake-up call. He rolled out of bed, showered, and checked out of the hotel without eating. He thought of driving by the office, but he needed to get back to San Francisco. Everything else could wait.

At the airport, he put up with the usual antiterrorist probing and poking, and boarded a 9:00 AM flight. He arrived without incident in San Francisco, and then called Dominique.

"How did it go?" asked Dominique.

"OK. I just flew in. I'll be at Antonio's in an hour. You remember Antonio."

"Of course," said Dominique. "He kept hitting on my friend Lisa, remember?"

"She was all over him."

"Please."

"Well, I'll be there in an hour or so. Tania is there now. Can you meet me at Antonio's this afternoon?"

"Of course."

"See you then. Missed you."

"Me too."

A cab pulled up to the curb. The driver got out and putted around on a dark wooden cane. The driver drove north, taking the Port of San Francisco exit and racing up 6th Street. Bent figures lurched into traffic, crossing the street haphazardly. "Gimme Shelter" played on the radio.

Ray took a call on his cell. Richard Perry's voice burbled with muted excitement: "He's at home now. We confirmed it. 110 Hayward, Apartment 4."

Ray hesitated. "OK, keep an eye on him. I'll be over there in a half-hour." He called Dominique and told her he would be late.

Ray directed the cab to the Sutter Street garage, where he

got out and had his car pulled around front. He drove south again toward the onramps for the Bay Bridge. Less heralded than her red sister, the Golden Gate, the Bay Bridge opened herself to all, her four silver towers planted in city soil, clamped down over the Embarcadero, running over SOMA. You could travel alongside the raw metal, drive around the towers, scramble up her sides. Set off against the downtown towers, the bridge looked like a long steel arm embracing the twin cities of Oakland and San Francisco.

He was over the bridge in seven minutes, weaving from lane to lane. He took the exit for the waterfront and headed towards the Oakland Coliseum. He stopped in front of a long row of stucco houses. They were designed to look like bungalows, with low red tile roofs and sheltered doorways. But after years of neglect, the homes had a grimy, sullen aspect, with doorways choked with debris, the red tile roof cracked and broken. Ray passed by a gray Honda with tinted windows—Richard Perry.

Ray pulled to the curb. Kids played on the weedy lawn next door, cracking a whiffle ball into high arcs over the street. Hip hop music played from somewhere. Oil stains glistened on the asphalt.

He headed toward the building complex. A plastic banner hung outside: "First Month Free!" Rusty air conditioners sagged from windows over greenish brown lumps that had once been shrubs. As he walked through the complex, Ray grimaced at the smell of soy sauce coming from a trash barrel. He opened a screen door to apartment 4 and knocked.

A voice inside: "Who is it?"

"Hey Bobby. Wondering if I could talk with you for a few minutes."

"Who are you?"

"I'm an investigator," said Ray. "Not a cop."

Silence. "I'm busy."

"It'll just take a few minutes. Talk about your work."

"You a cop?"

"No."

"I'm not interested."

"You may get interested. I know about the warrants, Bobby. As I said, I'm not a cop. Let's just talk, you and me, see if we can sort through a few things."

Silence from the door. Half a minute passed. Then Ray heard bolts being drawn back, the rattle of chains, a heavy thump on the floor. Then the door opened and Bobby Cherry's head peeked out. His skin looked translucent, the blue piping of his veins visible in his neck and hands. Eyes too close together, bulging slightly, amphibious and unreflective. He had an angry hole for a mouth.

"I'm looking into something that happened in San Francisco a few years ago," said Ray.

"Who ay' workin' for?"

"Me. I'm working on a special project." He scanned Cherry's face. A mustiness wafted from inside the apartment. "Can we sit down?"

Cherry shrugged.

"Let's talk for a minute." Ray stepped toward the door. Cherry hesitated, looked as if he would object. But he was still a Southerner with a modicum of politeness. Ray was inside before Cherry knew it.

Ray looked around at the living room. A World War II poster covered one wall; it blazed black and red, with a stylized Art Deco swastika merging into a black eagle flying over an army of helmeted, square-jawed German soldiers. A bookshelf with hate-spewing titles sat below the poster. Two folding chairs were set around a new, large-screen TV. People always splurged on TV, no matter what other necessities they had to forego. Cable TV was an American birthright.

Ray sat down in a chair. Cherry sat slowly, looking around his house as if he was seeing it for the first time.

"Where you from, Bobby?"

"Central Valley area," Cherry said calmly.

"How is the recruiting going?"

"Good." Cherry gave a bland smile.

"I'm curious. Why the wharf? How's the interest level among the tourists?"

"There's more than tourists there."

"I know," said Ray.

"How did you know we were there?" Cherry asked.

"We saw your affiliates there over the past few weeks. If the goofy-looking guy throws rocks at the seals again, someone might be leaning on him. Not me. But that's what I hear. Very active animal rights movement here."

Cherry guffawed and tried to look mean. He picked at his shirt, lifting invisible specks and dropping them on the floor.

"That wasn't my thing. I got nuthin' 'gainst a damn seal."

"I know. But why the wharf?"

"Ah, it's a good place," said Cherry. "It's legal for us to talk to people under the 1st Amendment, anyone and anywhere on public property. Freedom to associate. You can't stop us." Cherry tilted his head.

"You are right. But I'm not trying to stop you. I think your presentation should be seen by all." He paused. "Ever try North Beach?"

Cherry looked up. "No."

"That would be a good place. Lot of street traffic there too."

"We like the wharf."

"How about Oakland, the waterfront, maybe Jack London Square?"

Cherry said, "Too many Afros." Then he smiled, there was a little joke in there, that word, Afros.

"But you tried once, didn't you? Wasn't there a bit of an altercation?"

Cherry looked up and closed his eyes briefly. "Oakland's not our prime preferred territory."

"How long did you check out Powell Street?" Ray felt his blood race, and he forced a deep breath inside.

Cherry did not respond.

"Nice street, you'd like it. You know Powell Street," he said again, with no inflection of a question.

"I take Powell to the BART line there, downtown," said Cherry.

"But did you ever recruit in North Beach? Lots of Italians and Chinese there, not sure if that's your territory."

Cherry shook his head no, and smiled. "No Chinese allowed."

"But what about the Italians? Too dark probably. It's a funny thing, skin tone. I saw a bunch of Aryan Knights on TV talking about how dark-skinned Italians are considered niggers. Interesting. Southern Italians especially, Sicilians, Neapolitans. Too close to Africa not to have mixed blood with the black race. What's your thought on that matter? Could I join your group—I'm from Naples. Or am I just a nigger?"

Cherry shed a little half-smile, like he wasn't sure a full laugh was appropriate. Ray smiled back. "It's OK. I won't take offense."

"Ever see that movie?" said Cherry with a shady smile. "Dennis Hopper tells the godfather his grandma got fucked by niggers."

"That's a great scene," Ray said. "Walken calls him a cantaloupe. Nice play on the eggplant comment."

Cherry nodded, pointed to Ray. "I remember."

"Anyway, North Beach is an interesting place," said Ray. "We saw you there looking over the corner of Powell and Greenwich. What's so interesting about that intersection?"

Cherry's glee over the joke was gone and he looked serious. "Nothing."

"Who lives there, Bobby?"

"Don't know."

"You know the name. You were there before. Tell me about the corner apartment." He stepped close, putting his face near Cherry, just to the left. He felt very alive just then, a snake writhing in his gut.

"Just walking by," said Cherry. "Not sure—" Then he

stopped. His legs stretched out tautly in front of him, a bow waiting to be released.

"Tell me about the apartment. Who sent you there?"

Cherry's eyes moved around the room, insects looking for a crack.

"Who directed you to go to that apartment that one time? I know it wasn't you. Someone sent you there."

"No, I just walk by."

"How many times did they tell you to go there?"

"None. No one."

Ray felt flames wing along his neck and the surge almost ran the circuit. Stepping to the side, he flashed on an image of an elbow snapping into Cherry's head, the bony tip smacking the soft spot on the temple. Cherry making soft baby sounds and holding his busted skull.

But Ray just turned away, pushing back on the rage surging in his gut. He took a deep slow breath.

"Tell me about the bombing at that apartment."

"Don't know 'bout no bombing."

"Now we know that isn't true. All the White Aryan groups talked about it."

"Not with me." Cherry remained rigid.

"What do you think should happen to the person who bombed that apartment. How would you punish them?"

Cherry sat still in the same position. "Don't know. Depends on the evidence."

"I know you didn't plan it, design it. Bomb making is a specialized skill. But I want to hear it from you. Who else was involved. Who planned it. Who made the weapon. They used you to put it there, Bobby. That's the word on the street. You didn't even know what it was."

Ray put his voice into it. The room drummed in pulsing heat. Cherry looked at the floor again. Ray let the silence build, the room falling in on itself.

The men looked at each other. "I don't know nuthin' about no bombing," said Cherry sullenly. Then he shifted and resettled his bones.

"You were there," Ray began. "You delivered. Remember the name of the man who lived there? Infantino?" Cherry looked at him blankly.

"That's me. That was my apartment." Cherry's mouth began to work a bit. His eyebrows pinched in and up, the sclera of his eyeballs showing.

"All the evidence points to you. We have a witness, Bobby. She saw you, described you perfectly. And there's something else. Someone in your group is cutting a deal on a gun case. Major time. He's talking to the government about this thing in San Francisco. He's giving up lots of names. Yours was one. This is your time to sort this out. With only me here. You and I can work this out. By ourselves."

"I don' wanna talk no more," Cherry said. "I'll call — ".

"Bobby, you are not calling anyone." Ray stood up and walked around the room. A poster of an Aryan Knight caught his eye. This was not your typical white sheet and burning cross motif; this picture showed a knight in full armor astride a dapple-gray horse riding through a pristine forest clearing. His cloak was drawn back. The face was turned away, looking out toward a blazing gold horizon. Wording in the corner said "Protecting and Educating the Children of White America."

This was the new Aryan Knights: open, ecological, the white rangers protecting the trees. Ray smiled. "Look at this, Bobby. The new Aryan Knights takes care of its own. Impressive. It really is. More effective than anything else they've done in fifty years. They're like a family. Like a big daddy to little boys from fucked-up families."

Cherry launched a glance at Ray. Ray walked back to his chair and sat down. "Tell me about the South, Bobby. Where you from?"

Cherry said nothing.

"Alabama right? I love the South. This sounds funny, but the South is like New England in a weird way. No two areas of the country honor the past like New England and the Deep South. Patriots Day is a major deal in both places. In Boston, we shoot the Redcoats as they march through the fields in Lexington. Reenactments of the battle. 4th of July — massive fireworks in both places. In the South you've got the Confederate flag all over. Big Sunday dinners, just like New England."

Cherry looked tremendously disinterested.

"What was your father like?" Ray asked.

"What in the hell does this . . ." Cherry trailed off. He stared out the window.

"Southern fathers are like New England fathers: they commence with a whuppin' early on. Did your dad hit you when you were a kid?"

Cherry said nothing.

Ray walked behind Cherry. "My dad was tough. Medieval temperament. Spare the rod, spoil the child — that's the motto. He believed in the physical."

Ray sat down and moved his chair close. Cherry was scratching the back of his head now.

"Some fathers scare the shit outta their kids. Playing on the old fears. Black men who chased white girls behind the shed."

Cherry shook his head, frowning.

Teaching like that can cripple a young mind," Ray continued. "It happens everywhere. The limits of our parents. Passed on like a sickness, a disease. It sets in quick, Bobby. You were just a kid, and this guy is ripping out all your courage. Making you afraid. Probably a drinker too, wasn't he, sitting on his porch at night. Smashing you down so you felt as little as he did."

Ray saw Cherry go still.

He picked up a pamphlet. "So this is what you hand out.

Good design. Can you read this to me Bobby?"

Ray flicked over the pamphlet. Cherry stared and then shoved it away. "Of course I can read it."

"Your father never taught you to read, did he? A father like that, neglecting the schooling. Slave to the liquor. He probably snuck into the house at night when he was drunk, the back stairs creaking. You pretended you were asleep. Try to get through to morning. Fathers like that don't deserve the family they're given. Because when he was drinking, the worse came out."

Ray dropped off. "Do you have a sister?"

Cherry stirred ever so slightly, an animal whir.

"I know you do. Her name is Delana. Sisters. Man, you can't grow up with a mother and a sister and learn to hate women. Just not possible. You learn more from them than from any old book. No matter what your dad said. Or did. But some men fear the mystery of women. Soft and tough at the same time."

Ray stood up. "I know what happened there. Talked to some people, Bobby. Your family lived on Jefferson Street in Birmingham. Little house with blue trim and a screened porch. I saw it. Your neighbors, nice people. They were worried about you, the kids. They could hear him at night on the stairs, that heavy tread. The sound of a drunk father is the heaviest sound in the world."

Ray watched as Cherry tensed. "And you wanted to do something. You were ready. But you're a little kid. You're scared. Your dad going to your sister's room again. You thought about it, but never did anything. He's bigger. You were just a kid. Who do you tell, Bobby? What can you really do?"

Ray stopped. "And your mother, she should have known, why is daddy on the stairs to your sister's room again—"

Cherry rose out of the chair snarling, his mouth tight and wolfen. Ray cut the angle and stepped into him, getting inside. He drove his right fist through the middle of Cherry's face, chopping him down. Cherry crashed to the side and knocked a chair over. Ray wrapped an arm around Cherry's head and drove a knee into the side of Cherry's face. The muffled crunch of cartilage snapping. Drove the knee again. And again. Ray felt a storm of madness coming up inside, and knew he would kill Cherry here, just leave the fucking kid on the floor. But Cherry just sagged, all the fight run out of him. He whimpered on the floor. His face was a mess of snot and blood, his teeth stained red.

Ray regained control of his reflexes. He took a breath; this was not the way. Cherry and his sad little apartment were not the end of the line. The road only started here. "Tell me about the address."

Cherry moaned. "You diggin' 'bout my goddamn family! What the hell you doin'!" He fought for breath amid tears and blood.

"Bobby, take a minute." Cherry sat up and walked to a window, trying to regain his composure. "All this is not your fault." Ray sat down. "There's a rat inside your group. Someone high up. You know he won't do any time if he can sell a story about someone else doing this thing. That's how it works. He's selling a dream. And the cops are buying it. Someone else is gonna to do slow time on a federal rap. Someone low on the totem pole."

Cherry wiped his face with the back of his hand.

"It always works this way, Bobby. The old men sell out the younger guys who do the grunt work. They'll have the best lawyers in town so don't think you're ever gonna hear from them again. You know that's how it works. They ever come see you here in this apartment complex?" Bobby looked up and shook his head.

"You're just meat to them. I know you were involved, Bobby. I just need to know why. If you just delivered — and I think that's all you did — we can deal with that. If you planned the bombing, arranged the whole thing, that's a different story. But I don't think it was you who planned it."

Ray got up and touched Cherry's shoulder. "Was this an isolated thing? That time they asked you to do something like this?"

Cherry said nothing. Then he put his head down and looked at the floor. Ray stared at him and let the silence grow.

"First time," said Cherry.

"OK. How did you first learn of the address in North Beach?"

"They told me to drop off a package."

"Who did?"

"I just had the address—no names. That's all I knew." Cherry talked into the floor.

"Who told you?"

"It was Lee. At a meeting."

"Lee who."

"Lee Hightower. He runs it." Cherry wiped the snot off his face with his left hand.

"Where is Lee Hightower?"

Cherry looked down and rubbed his neck. "Outside San Diego. He runs the California squads." He struggled to sit up.

Ray knew Cherry was telling the truth; Hightower's organization was a well-known entity with longtime roots near San Diego. "Who was the bomb maker?" Ray asked.

"I don't know, man, I just took a package over, no names. I never knew what was in there."

"Well, how did you get it?"

"I went to one of the rallies. One night, we had a meeting and they told me to meet someone at Powell Street. Near the subway." Cherry's eyes were wide, hateful. "A guy gave me a gym bag."

Ray tilted his head, staring at Cherry. "How did he know you?"

"We met before, the rally was the night before?"

"What device was used?"

Cherry spread his hands but said nothing. Ray waited. "I thought it was a warning, just scare someone. I found out later it was live, a pipe bomb," said Cherry. "One foot long metal inside a PVC. The PVC was filled with nails and shit, all kinds of metal." Cherry looked at him, eyes almost pleading. "I never knew, sir. I swear I didn't."

Ray flashed to the grisly plasma mess on Powell, the detritus caused by jagged metal rocketing haphazardly through human flesh. He stood back. Cherry sat up, holding his face in his hands, breathing raggedly on the carpet. Rap music pulsed from the street.

Ray stood over him. "Now tell me all about Lee Hightower."

It was close to 4:00 PM when Ray finished with Cherry. He stood up and walked toward the door. The room felt cleaner, something released, a passing of some crawling horror. Then he turned. Cherry sat in a chair, slumped in the seat like he had been deboned of everything that was once alive in him.

"Thanks, Bobby," Ray said. "I appreciate you being honest. I really do." He opened the door and the sunlight slashed into the darkened room. "I may have to talk with you again." Then he stepped outside and slammed the door behind him.

Chapter 32

Ray drove back in silence to San Francisco. The East Bay sun gave way to drifts of gray sky. The afternoon traffic was slow. He mulled over the name Lee Hightower. He knew Hightower was involved with several San Diego hate groups, but the extent of his role had been unclear. Hightower was a bigger player than expected. A new line to pursue.

The sky blanketed the city in gray. Ray pulled up to Antonio's house, and walked up the front walk. He entered the living room where Antonio and Tania were sitting. Tania wore olive-colored cotton pants that fit her well, along with a black blouse. Silver bracelets adorned her wrists.

Dominique walked in from the hall, looking elegant in a cream-colored business suit.

"I'm back," he said, drawing out the words. He walked to Dominique and held her, kissed her. Then he exchanged greetings with Antonio and Tania, and settled in a chair. Tania sat quietly, impenetrable.

He looked at Dominique. "I hope Antonio made introductions."

"Of course," Dominique said, smiling at Tania.

"I met Victoria last night," Ray said.

Tania stirred and looked up in surprise. "How did you manage that?" she asked.

"I showed up at her house."

"Just like that?" Tania asked.

"He's been doing that for years," said Dominique. "Cute the first time. Now it's just irritating."

"No one can resist a navy blue pinstripe suit."

"What did she do when you showed up?" asked Tania.

"She made me wait a bit, showing me who's boss. She

heard me out but she admitted nothing. We talked—or I talked—and she acted like I was speaking Bulgarian."

"What was your impression of her?" asked Dominique.

"She does not disappoint. Impressive. Strong as a buffalo. Comes off as bloodless, cruel. All that coiled power hidden by a pianist's hands and a face that looks embalmed. I don't know what she took out of the meeting. I tried to push her on the exposure she faces from her reliance on Lucas."

"Do you think she buys it?" asked Dominique.

"It won't phase her," interrupted Tania.

"She's not happy about what happened," said Ray, looking at Tania. "But I'm not sure what she's going to do about it."

"We should talk to the DA about conspiracy to murder charges against Lucas." said Dominique. "Victoria won't like a bright light shining on someone that close to her."

"Can your office reach out to someone there?"

"Of course. I'll start on it this afternoon." She walked with Ray toward the door. Once they were out of sight of the others, she stopped and stared at Ray. "Are you OK? You look amped up."

"Something happened on the other case," said Ray. "The guy in the East Bay I told you about. I'll fill you in later."

"OK. I called my friend who gave me that breakdown on the Triad," Dominique said. "The triad is not just moving drugs anymore."

"What else?"

"Remember the snake heads? Syndicates get girls from Russia or Estonia. They either work off debts, knowing they are going to be slaves working on their backs for years. Or they get tricked into it. Ads about working in Germany for a British couple. Once the girls cross the border, the gangs seize their passports and they work.

"The Black Fist has upped the game. The Mexican border is not just for immigrants or prostitutes. They have done those runs for years. Last year, the Border Patrol began to pick up some Arabs on the border. They were dressed like Mexicans and for a while, no one even noticed. But an Arabic speaking agent— there was such a guy there, if you can believe it— heard two men talking. They are being debriefed now. They appear highly trained and are resisting any interrogation techniques practiced at the border."

"They're smuggling terrorists into the country on the old drug routes," said Ray, shaking his head.

"Yes. Makes sense. No one has a better smuggling system than the Triad. So now the terrorists are subcontracting out their transport to the Triad. Chinese gangs have perfected penetrating U.S. borders—why not use the best?"

Ray was silent. "Subcontracting terrorism."

"So now you can see why they want Tania. Cho's group has the best connection to the Arabs. If the feds pressure her, and she mentions the Triad link, news spreads about their work for terrorists. Then it's a whole new level of attention on them."

"I have to run," said Dominique. She pressed his hand and kissed him. "Lots to think about."

Ray walked back into the living room. Tania gave him a curious look. "She's pretty. How long have you known her?"

"Many years. We've known each other since law school." That Tania was interested in his relationship with Dominique gave him a feeling of cheap teenage satisfaction.

"I like her. Smart lady," said Tania.

"Yes, she is."

"So what's next?"

"What's next," said Ray, "is that we wait. Victoria probably got the news of Lucas's North Beach session, and I have to think that will disappoint her. We'll see."

Tania nodded and stared at her feet. "While you were gone, I spoke with Moon."

"You called her?" Ray asked.

"She called me."

"Is she OK?"

"Yes, she's fine."

"What happened after Marin?" Ray asked.

"She said she was at the front door when you drove behind the building. After we left, those guys carried the bodies of a couple men to the car and took off. Police arrived a few minutes later."

"Anyone come after her?"

"They never bothered her," said Tania. "She never spoke with them."

"She notice any of them following her?"

"No, she didn't mention it," Tania replied, an edge to her voice. She brushed her hair back and looked at Ray. "I want to see her."

"Soon," said Ray.

"I don't see why it's such a problem."

"If they followed her already, they'll stay on her. Keep her under surveillance."

"I need to see her," Tania said. "She needs help!"

Ray sat down heavily in a chair near the window. He stared outside. Alcatraz jutted a rocky forehead into the gray water of San Francisco Bay as seagulls whirled in the cold air. Treasure Island boldly green; Sausalito a smoky mirage across the harbor.

Tania sat holding a book, her mouth set. Ray was again struck by the contrast between her angelic face and gutty personality. He shook himself. "What were you reading?"

"One of Antonio's books. A movie guide on old westerns."

They sat quietly for a while.

"Why don't you call Moon and tell her we'll pick her up at 4:00 today. You can call her on my cell phone and tell her where to meet us."

Tania looked relieved. "Thank you. You have no idea how important this is to me."

"Make sure I have her number, OK?"

Ray got up and walked into his room. He opened a window, and lay down on the bed. The machinery of the hunt was clanking to a rhythm he had not set. He hated waiting, and had no intention of rotting while Victoria moved. But how long could he hide Tania? People tended to focus on familiar dangers, while unknown demons inched closer, closer, bold approach making them invisible to the obsessive eye. What did he really know about this underworld of money-laundering massage parlors, illegal card games, dead-eyed young men hustling to midnight meetings?

He drifted off, waking later to a soft, polite knocking.

"Come in."

Tania entered. "I called Moon. It's all set for 4:00 PM. Here's her number."

"What did she say?"

"She's worried. The stuff in Marin shook her up." Tania smiled. "I'm excited to see her."

"How about this old boyfriend of yours, Steven? Did Moon ever meet him?"

"Yes."

"They get along?"

"I guess. I don't think they had any problems. Why do you ask?"

"She told me differently."

Tania frowned. "Well, maybe she felt protective of me. Steven could be weird."

"How?" He thought of Steven entering the Lexus on Jones Street.

"Guys can get weird," said Tania. "They come off very detached at first, after they find out what you do. They say that they want you to live your own life. But they get possessive. But it never got out of hand with Steven."

"Steven wasn't like that?"

"He was a nice guy. He even smelled naive. Like he was doused in baby powder."

Ray laughed. "I'll go pick up Moon."

JOHN F. NARDIZZI

Chapter 33

Ray headed to the car and drove west over Telegraph Hill. On Van Ness, he dodged an SUV pulling out from the curb, some puffball struggling to pilot his craft, his lone weekly exertion.

He drove on. He took a right on Pine Street, chewing up intersection after intersection as he hit a jackpot of green lights. A rainbow blur of Victorian homes lined the street, painted in wild patterns of mauve, purple, amber and gold. An old lady sat on a porch and watched the traffic.

He dialed the telephone number he had been given for Moon.

"Hi Moon. It's Ray."

"Hi."

"Are you at home?"

"Yes."

"Let's do this discreetly. Take a cab and tell him to drive straight up Divisadero, then left on Fulton. Head up Divisadero and pull over near the entrance to USF."

"OK. Where will you be?"

"I'll call your cell again in fifteen minutes."

He hung up and headed west on Pine, jostling for position as he crossed Geary. He passed the Peace Pagoda in Japantown. Traffic was building to heart-attack levels. He turned left on Divisadero, racing through the Fillmore. The sweet smell of a barbecue joint spiced the air near Grove and Divisadero. He took a right on Fulton. After a few minutes, he arrived in front of the hilltop campus of the University of San Francisco, and pulled over to the side of the street. He watched the entrance. A coed in tight jeans squeezed her way up a steep pathway toward the campus. Thank god for the hills, Ray thought.

A cab pulled over next to a long path winding up the hill.

He sat and watched. No other cars pulled over. No sinister movements on the grassy knoll.

He dialed Moon.

"Moon. Is that you parked?"

"Yes."

"Start walking back to Divisadero. I'll call you in a few minutes."

A pause on the line. "OK."

Ray watched as Moon exited the cab, her hair pulled back to reveal her perfect porcelain neck. She looked sleek and untouchable, dressed in a hip-length white sweater, black pants, black boots, and aviator sunglasses. She briefly scanned the horizon, and then walked down the hill toward Fulton.

He watched her as she strode, graceful but quick. Then he called her again.

"Moon, cross Fulton and take a cab straight down toward the beach."

She flagged a cab and zoomed up Fulton. No one followed. Citizens went about their business in the emerging sun.

Ray pulled into traffic. The cab was easy to follow—a decrepit wreck painted a puke-tan color, with rusty holes near one wheel well. The driver proceeded at a leisurely pace toward the ocean.

He called again.

"Have the cabby drive up to Geary."

A few moments later, the cab turned right, sagging on the turn. Ray followed several car lengths behind.

Ray watched Moon's petite head in the back seat, bouncing in sync with potholes in the road. They passed Mel's Drive-In, its tasty cool-blue neon drawing all eyes. He called Moon again.

"Moon, have the cabby bang a U-turn and drop you off at the corner near Mel's." The cab slowed, and took the left.

The scrambling had smoked out anyone tailing them. He followed the cab, keeping a sharp eye on any other cars. No one made any quick turns.

A red Lexus pulled up quickly behind him. Ray noted an Asian male driver. The Lexus turned left on Euclid. He relaxed.

Moon was paying the cabby and looking across Geary. Ray zoomed up and stopped in front of her. She appeared mildly irritated at being rustled all over the city.

Moon got in, looking at Ray. He pulled away. The pulse and flow of traffic, people running in front of cars on a million afternoon errands.

Ray made a couple of quick turns, tires chirping mildly. He drove up a side street. No one was tailing them, and he felt more comfortable.

"Sorry for the chaos," he said. "I had to take a few precautions, as I'm sure you can understand."

"Yes," she said. Up close, she looked more attractive than he'd remembered, even if windswept.

"Tania is looking forward to seeing you. The last few days have been tough for her."

"I miss her. Thanks for picking me up."

They drove on in silence through the redwoods and eucalyptus of the Presidio. He took a right on Union Street and drove through Pacific Heights.

Ray aimed the car up Russian Hill, stopping for a cable car at Powell Street. Tourists hung off the sides of the cable car like baboons. Outside a store, a grocer built a pyramid of oranges on a green cart. A few oranges rolled off the cart and meandered down the hill.

They zipped through North Beach, and pulled into the garage on Kearny.

Ray and Moon entered a side door, and stepped into a hallway. Ray guided her toward the living room. Antonio came in wearing bright shorts and a black T-shirt. Ray introduced Moon to Antonio.

"Let me know if you need anything," said Antonio. "A drink, whatever you want."

Ray and Moon entered the living room. Tania sat on the

sofa, still reading a book. She looked up and rose quickly. She looked relaxed, even restored. The two women embraced. They stood that way for some time, letting the fear of the last few days slip from their bones, standing in a sunny spot.

"I'll leave you two for a while," said Ray. He exited the living room. In a way, he envied their closeness. They both intrigued him, their sleek black hair, the circular way they approached conversation, spiraling slowly, sparrows over a forest.

In the kitchen, Ray and Antonio read the newspaper.

"Jesus, two beautiful women," said Antonio. "What are you doing in here with me?"

Ray poured a glass of Cabernet. The label showed a masked horseman clad in red. "This looks expensive," he said. "Your taste is developing."

Antonio grunted.

In the living room, the two women held each other, speaking in hushed tones.

"I missed you," said Tania.

"I know. Me too."

"The last two days. All these surreal revelations," said Tania. "I feel trapped in this house." Tania held Moon's face in her hands, kissed her lips, her forehead. "It's been so long, Moon!"

"I can't believe this is happening to us," said Moon quietly.

"But how are you?" Tania leaned forward to look into Moon's face.

"OK, given the circumstances." Moon whispered, "I didn't know if I could trust him. He showed up asking about you."

"I know. That seems to be how he works. He burst in on me too," said Tania, pulling Moon closer. "But he's legit. I would be dead by now if—"

Moon moved away, looking exhausted. Her hands trembled slightly.

"You poor thing," said Tania.

"You look as bad as I do," said Moon.

"I want to end this crazy life," said Tania. "How long can we keep hiding?" Tania put her face in her hands.

Moon moved to her, holding her, stroking her hair. "We don't have to do it much longer," she said softly.

"Promise me you will stay with me. Don't go away."

"I'm staying," said Moon. "This time forever." She leaned close. "We can leave tonight—we need to."

Tania looked up. "What? How can we leave—"

"They came after me," Moon whispered. "This was after Marin." She hung her head. "They did things to me." She lifted her shirt sleeve. Tania looked with horror at the splotches of mottled burns, a mess of raw red tissue. A sob convulsed Moon's body and then subsided.

"I didn't say anything," she whispered. "I never gave them anything—"

"Oh my god, Moon, what did they do to you! You need help—"

"They wanted me to take them to you. But I would never do that. I tricked them." She was crying. "They thought I was on their side after they did this. They gave me a phone to call them once we met. They said they would take us away from Ray, that he's up to something. I told them I would call. But I never would!" She grabbed Tania's hand. "I just want us to be together."

Tania sprang up. "Did you ever call them?"

"Never! They called me but—"

"They can track us with these phones!" Tania raced toward the kitchen, pulling Moon behind her.

Ray heard a crash under the kitchen floor. Antonio looked up. "The basement door!" Ray ran toward the hallway as Tania burst through the door.

"Ray, they're here! They followed her here, they tracked a cell phone—"

"I'll get the shotgun!" yelled Antonio. He rushed out.

"Get upstairs!" Ray said to Tania. Drawing his gun, he led the way back into the hallway toward the stairs.

They were too late. On the right, the basement door burst open. Two black-clad Asian men swept into the alcove, covering the kitchen with shotguns. They blasted off two, three shots, and a tremendous roar echoed in the room. Ray shoved Tania toward the hallway stairs. Unloaded five rounds at the men as they raced into the kitchen. Wild gunfire exploded around him. Bullets punctured holes in the plaster. Already down to a few shots. Then he dove behind the thick wood walls of the dining room.

He heard feet scrambling on the stairs—Tania and Moon seemed to be out of the way. But he heard a once-vital female voice braying its distress.

Where was Antonio? Ray looked around. They were coming. Dining room wrapped into the kitchen—the shooters could enter from either way. But they didn't know the layout. Better bring the attack and hope that Antonio covered the back.

He aimed the gun toward the rear doorway in the dining room. Then he began to crawl silently toward the kitchen.

A shot cracked behind him—Antonio crouching on the stairs and firing round after round into the kitchen. A hurricane of noise and mayhem. Something crashed into the stove. Pots clattered on the floor. Ray got up and ran toward the doorway. A figure in black was backing in, distracted by the shotgun flak. The figure whirled. Five feet away, Ray fired repeatedly—push, hold, squeeze. The rhythmic concussions echoed off the walls. The man toppled back in rude punctuation to the blasts. He lay still.

Antonio was calling for him. Ray raced back to the foyer. At the foot of the stairs he saw Moon sprawled on the floor, unmoving. Blood flowed from her neck. Tania was crumpled near the stairs, eyes closed, breathing raggedly.

Antonio and Ray scrambled on the floor, pulling blankets on Tania and Moon. Antonio called 911. A heavy smell of smoke in the air. Ray felt fury run over his limbs. He thought of Victoria Chang's cryptic response. This was done at her bidding, the emblem of her black design all over it.

He crawled to Tania, holding her tightly. The blue carpet was turning into a slick, damp swamp of blood. Antonio drifted from room to room, checking on Moon and Tania, yelling instructions into the phone.

He had swooped into California just a few days ago. He played his hand boldly, the confrontation in Cambridge. But now he sat once again amidst carnage in an apartment on a hill in San Francisco. He held Tania, listening for sirens, his heartbeat loud in his ears.

Chapter 34

The two-tone Lexus, squat and luxurious in its deliberate pace, motored through the afternoon traffic on Geary. Behind the tinted windows, Lucas Michaels peered out at the traffic. His hands tapped the imported wood inlay of the steering wheel. A Sade CD played. He believed that such music added an exotic tint to his personal aura, a scent he could somehow emit, an unexpected compliment to his patrician profile.

The past few days had veered close to being a professional disaster for him. The Marin matter was botched. The ridiculous meeting in North Beach was an embarrassment. The situation had dragged on much too long. In just a few weeks, the missing girl had grown into a cancer. Once he had found her, Ray Infantino had been a good deal more effective — and intrusive — than anticipated. All this had caused an unfortunate backwash on his reputation.

Victoria had made her displeasure known, and he knew that thirty years of a business partnership were crumbling. But in the end, they had worked things out. He had received word that the matter was to be handled by an old consort of Tania's — a woman no less.

But Tania had again survived the attack. He had not pressed for details.

It occurred to him again that, by the end of his career, he had engaged in acts that would have warped his soul as a younger man. The idealism of youth. He stifled the urge to ruminate. He had made a choice a long time ago, and the rewards had been significant. He understood that the dead make poor editors. History is for the victors, and he would be victorious here. That was the crucial thing. It was time to press on to new business.

He ignored the unpleasant swirling in his gut, and concentrated on the road.

At a red light he watched a young girl in white knee-high socks stroll by, creating a minor riot among a scrap of teenaged boys. He got a sense of pounding music, hip-hop, urban poses, kids in warm-up jackets, gold and red.

A silver BMW angled from his left and slid expertly in front of him. He frowned — as a rule, BMW drivers were arrogant pricks. He watched people on the sidewalk, streaming past bakeries and shops with awnings covered in bird dung.

An abrupt movement on his left. An Asian man in sunglasses appeared, tight in his window. Lucas felt a pit in his belly. The man raised a gun, pointed it at Lucas's temple, fired pointblank. A fiery roar ate his face, blood splashing merrily over the leather interior.

The shooter turned to the nearest restaurant, the Bangkok Café, and fired several shots into the front window. Bullets pocked the glass and snapped into the wall. A diner dove for cover behind a potted palm tree. An old man reflexively stood up, jarring his table; hot soup spilled on his lap. He howled in pain.

The shooter took off through the stalled cars on Geary. On the street, people scattered. The brave and the fools looked around, confused, not sure of what they saw. A young couple on the sidewalk pointed to the restaurant, certain that the shots had come from the long-haired white dude at table four.

Who can tell what happens in three lanes of traffic at rush hour?

Lucas's body folded into the steering wheel. His foot slipped off the brake. The Lexus rolled forward, just another car now, and crashed into a hydrant. Water surged upwards in a geyser, and a misty confusion rolled through the San Francisco streets.

Chapter 35

The ambulance arrived, men and women in medical blues. The technicians hunched over Tania. They made brisk movements with the shiny steel gadgetry of emergencies. Tubes, beeping machines, oxygen tanks, and old fashioned stuff as well—towels, rubber gloves and blankets. Ray heard Tania moan.

One technician walked over to Moon. He checked her pulse, and wrapped her in the blanket. She had lost a lot of blood.

Cops filled the room. A detective in a gray suit stood with a pen in hand, interviewing Antonio. He glanced at the women, nodding grimly.

Ray spoke for forty-five minutes to two detectives. Then a technician approached, a dark man with short hair, Indian maybe, neat and cool. "They're gonna be OK, sir." He nodded toward Tania. "She took a bullet in the back. She is in some pain, but she's OK." Ray nodded dimly.

"You know the other girl had burn marks on her?"

Ray shook his head no. "How recent?"

"A few days or so. Her arms are real bad." The EMT moved away. "We'll take care of your friends."

"Thank you."

He hated hospitals. He thought again of Diana and the ambulances that rushed to the apartment after the bombing. There had been no need to take anyone to a hospital that day. Everyone was dead. He tried to relax, but his lungs felt heavy and compressed. He sat on the edge of a chair and tried to breathe deeply.

Antonio by his side. "Jesus, what a couple of days for you."

Ray sat mutely. So many deserved a payback. He ground his palm into his knuckles, feeling the bone.

Later that night, he sat in the hospital room, his heavy

brown leather jacket across his lap. The windows were open. Stars speckled the black sky. The sad, steady bleating of the monitors the only sound. Tania's upper back was wrapped in a bandage. She had slept all evening. He looked at her fine brown hand, now marred with tubes running in her veins. She looked peaceful as she slept.

Her eyes opened. Her hands tapped the sheet as if she wasn't sure where she was.

"Tania, how do you feel?"

"Thirsty." Her voice was faint. "Can I have water?" She fingered the bandages at her back.

"The doctors said you can't drink or eat for a while. The tubes have to do it for you."

"Moon brought those men accidentally," Tania said. "Her phone — they tampered with it."

Ray nodded. "GPS."

"What happened?" Tania asked.

He hesitated.

"Where is Moon?" Tania looked up. Her eyes, brown as fallen oak leaves, searched his face.

"She's here, Tania. But she was hit."

"Where?"

"Her neck. They have her in intensive care too." Tania sank into the bed, her back arching, sending the monitors crazy. Ray held on to her hand. Tania's eyes closed and she grimaced. She turned her back toward him, sobbing. After a few minutes, she lay still, a small lump in the sheets.

"I just want to go. It's never going to end, is it?" she said.

"I'm sorry Tania for what happened. But even these people tire of the chase. They will move on when they see new threats to their businesses." He sat there looking at the stars, listening to the television drone. Footsteps in the hallway. Voices at the nurses station.

Tania kept her back to him, hunched into her pillow. Ray sat there, a shape in the darkness. He put his hand on her shoulder. She didn't pull away. Eventually Tania fell asleep.

"I'm not going anywhere," he said.

The next morning he left the hospital before Tania awoke. He walked to the lobby and called Dominique. He asked her to meet him at Coit Tower. Then he hailed a cab and headed east toward Telegraph Hill. A morning fog drifted inland and everything looked dingy, smeared with gray. He got out at the statue honoring Christopher Columbus in Pioneer Park, just below the elegant gray tower.

A few minutes later, Dominique stepped out of a cab. She walked up the steps to where Ray sat on a cement wall, and they embraced, holding each other.

"I heard what happened," she said. "Both her and Lucas."

"Lucas found out how gangs lay off middle managers." Ray stared into the mist. "Someone got to Moon. They tortured her. Burn marks all over her arms. They put software on her phone that activated her GPS. Took them right to Tania." He shook his head.

"You couldn't know that," said Dominique.

"I should have anticipated it." Ray shook his head. "This hill, right now, I hate it." He pulled his leather coat closed. "It's just like before." Dominique started to say something but stopped short.

"How is Tania?" she asked.

"OK," Ray said. "Moon is in bad shape though. Tania was distraught when she heard."

"Of course."

"There's so much unfinished business here," said Ray.

"I know."

"You and I also," Ray said. "It meant a lot being back here with you."

She smiled, moved into him. "Thanks for saying that."

"I mean that." He looked out across the bay. "I'm going to stay a while, try to make sure that Tania gets some help. Put her in a place where they can't find her."

"Where's that?" she asked.

"I don't know yet. I'll have to find a way to get her out

of here. I know someone who remakes people, helps them disappear. Gangs focus on clear dangers. We need to make them come to the end of caring. Like they did with Lucas."

"How did it go with the other case?"

"OK." Ray set his face into the wind. "Got some good information. But I wanted this kid Cherry to be the guy. I felt it."

"Was he what you expected?"

"He admitted he delivered the bomb. Says others organized it. A group out of San Diego. He didn't want to tell me. But what I took from him—" Ray paused. "It didn't feel like I thought it would."

"How so?"

"Dreaming of revenge. Thinking it would fill the pit. Then you look around and you're just digging to bury yourself right beside the first hole."

Ray put his arm around Dominique and pulled her into him. They looked across the cold sea. The sun rose, and the wind swirled orange swaths above boats rising and falling on the currents.

THE END

⊂ʒ୫ɔ

TELEGRAPH HILL

CPSIA information can be obtained at www.ICGtesting.com
Printed in the USA
BVOW03s0632110913

330843BV00005B/20/P